# NO DOUBT ABOUT IT, THEY'RE THE VERY BEST!

Some of the record breakers in this book are the great names and teams from the past. Others are as new as today's sports pages—superstars you love to see as they set new marks every time they take the field. Whoever they are, you can be sure they are the fastest, the toughest, and the most successful players ever known to the game! Join these amazing superstars for some exciting gridiron action as they smash old records and set up new ones of their own. You're not going to believe the things these football players have done in their exciting careers. Find out all about the best—

## PRO FOOTBALL'S RECORD BREAKERS!

**Books by Bill Gutman**

GREAT MOMENTS IN BASEBALL
GREAT MOMENTS IN PRO FOOTBALL
PRO FOOTBALL'S RECORD BREAKERS
REFRIGERATOR PERRY
STRANGE AND AMAZING BASEBALL STORIES
STRANGE AND AMAZING FOOTBALL STORIES
STRANGE AND AMAZING WRESTLING STORIES

Available from ARCHWAY Paperbacks

Sports Illustrated

# PRO FOOTBALL'S
# RECORD
# BREAKERS

## Bill Gutman

AN ARCHWAY PAPERBACK
Published by POCKET BOOKS • NEW YORK

Photographs courtesy of *Sports Illustrated:* Andy Hayt: p. 49;
John Iacono: p. 71; Walter Iooss Jr.: pp. 31, 116; Heinz
Kluetmeier: p. 87; Neil Leifer: pp. 26, 65, 93; Manny Millan: p.
119; Bill Smith: p. 75; Tony Tomsic: pp. 3, 8; Jerry Wachter: p.
42. Photos on pages 61, 79, 104, 109, 111 courtesy of AP/Wide
World Photos.

AN ARCHWAY PAPERBACK *Original*

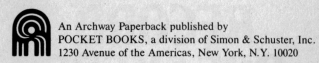

An Archway Paperback published by
POCKET BOOKS, a division of Simon & Schuster, Inc.
1230 Avenue of the Americas, New York, N.Y. 10020

ISBN: 0-671-64375-4

First Archway Paperback printing September 1987

10 9 8 7 6 5 4 3 2

AN ARCHWAY PAPERBACK and colophon are
registered trademarks of Simon & Schuster, Inc.

SPORTS ILLUSTRATED is a registered trademark
of Time Inc.

Printed in U.S.A.

IL 4+

# Contents

# The Day Simms Was Super

For Phil Simms, recognition has come hard. Playing in an era of outstanding young quarterbacks, the New York Giants' blond-haired signalcaller has never been considered·among the elite at his position. Ask a football fan in the mid-1980s about the top QB's and the names you're likely to hear are Montana, Marino, Elway, O'Brien, Kosar, Esiason, McMahon, and perhaps one or two others.

But few people would mention Phil Simms. There were skeptics the minute the Giants made Simms their number-one draft choice in 1979. Phil who? was the popular call. After all, Simms was coming out of little Morehead State College. How good could he really be in the big bad NFL, where many people still believe that only the big names from the big schools can make it big?

And, indeed, it took Phil Simms some time. The Giants tried to ease him into the lineup. But once he got a chance to play, it seemed he couldn't stay healthy.

He was hurt in 1981 and his backup, Scott Brunner, led the team into the playoffs. A pre-season injury benched him for the strike-shortened 1982 campaign. And when new coach Bill Parcells picked Brunner over Simms at the beginning of the '83 season, more people than ever said that the club had wasted that first pick back in '79.

Another injury in '83 didn't help Simms' image. Then in 1984, he finally won the starting job and at the same time had an injury-free season. The team finished at 9–7, won a playoff game against the Rams, then lost to eventual Super Bowl winner San Francisco. A year later, Simms led the club to a 10–6 season and yet another trip to the playoffs, a wild-card victory, and then a loss to the Bears, the super team of 1985.

During this period, the Giants were building a strong club, characterized by a rock-ribbed defense that was considered second only to that of the Chicago Bears. The offense was something less formidable, though in 1985, Joe Morris emerged as one of the top running backs in the league.

As for Phil Simms, he was beginning to hang up some very healthy numbers. Yet because the defense was considered the heart of the team, Simms still wasn't recognized as a leader or a top-notch quarterback. Too erratic, some said. Can't win the big one, trumpeted others. Injury prone, still others said, though Phil had just completed his second straight season without missing a game.

So in 1986, Phil Simms still felt he had something to prove. And this time he was surrounded by a group of

**Phil Simms of the New York Giants was unreal in Super Bowl XXI. He completed a record-breaking 22 of 25 passes against Denver, many coming despite intense pressure from the Bronco defense.**

outstanding football players. It was the defense, especially the linebackers, and halfback Joe Morris who continued to get most of the publicity. The linebackers, led by Lawrence Taylor, Harry Carson, and Carl Banks, were the most punishing group in the league. Halfback Morris was thought to be the hub around which the offense was built.

When the team began winning early, the defense and

Morris got most of the credit. Simms was playing well, but injuries to several of his pass receivers, including top threat Lionel Manuel, didn't help. Then, in mid-season, the quarterback went into a slump and it was indeed Morris and the defense that carried the team.

In a game against Dallas, Simms could only manage six completions in 18 tries for 67 yards. Yet Morris ran for 181 yards and the defense recovered three fumbles as the club won, 17–14.

"I had been very tentative prior to that game," Simms admitted. "I was looking not to make mistakes. When you do that, you're trying not to lose. It was a real distraction to me, and it caused the coaches to alter our play calling. That made it tough.

"But after the Dallas game Coach Parcells called me aside. He told me he still thought I was great and told me how he wanted me to play. From that point on, I threw better. I threw the ball aggressively. My attitude had changed."

The club took its final seven games to win the NFC Eastern Division with an impressive 14–2 mark. They were in the playoffs again. Only this time, they were given a good chance to go to their first Super Bowl, and win their first NFL championship in 30 years.

In the NFC divisional playoff, the Giants wiped out the tough San Francisco 49ers, 49–3. Simms had a fine day, but the defense grabbed the headlines, shutting down the powerful Niner attack and putting quarterback Joe Montana out of the game.

Then in the NFC title game, it was again the defense

that prevailed, shutting out the Washington Redskins, 17–0. The victory put the Giants into Super Bowl XXI, where they would be facing the explosive Denver Broncos. The Broncos were led by one of the outstanding young quarterbacks in the NFL, John Elway. In the AFC title game, Elway made headlines by driving the Broncos 98 yards in the closing seconds, enabling the club to tie the Cleveland Browns and send the game into overtime. Elway then led his club to victory and into the Super Bowl.

So Phil Simms was once again playing second fiddle. Because of the ease with which the Giants whipped the 49ers, and the intense wind conditions in their NFC title tiff with the Redskins, Simms had only thrown a total of 33 passes in both games, completing 16 for 226 yards. Modest stats. But he had thrown for five touchdowns with no interceptions. Yet none of that prepared anyone for the record-breaking performance Phil Simms was about to deliver in Super Bowl XXI.

The game was played on January 25, 1987, at the huge Rose Bowl in Pasadena, California. And as the two teams warmed up, Phil Simms sensed that it might be his day.

"Sometimes you get in a groove," Simms said, "and I felt like that all week before the game. Then, when I was warming up, I really sensed it. I told everyone, 'I got it today. I can put it in there.' Our offense had a lot to prove. Nobody had said anything about us all week."

So Phil Simms stepped out on center stage in perhaps the single biggest spectacle in all of sports and went to work. Denver drew first blood when Rich Karlis kicked a 48-yard field goal early in the game. But then Simms showed what he meant when he said he was in a groove.

He drove the Giants 78 yards for their first touchdown. On the drive, he was perfect, connecting on six straight passes for 69 yards. The TD came on a six-yard strike to tight end Zeke Mowatt. New York fans thought their team was on the way.

But Denver's Elway came right back with a drive of his own. He matched Simms' drive with a six for six performance, and finally ran it over on a quarterback draw. The kick made it a 10-7 Denver game at the 12:54 mark of the first period.

In the second quarter, the defenses tightened. The Giants lived up to their reputation by making a rockribbed goal-line stand, as the Broncos tried, strangely, to run it in. Bronco kicker Karlis missed a pair of field goals, and the Giants forced a safety when veteran end George Martin tackled Elway in his own end zone. That made it 10-9.

The second quarter was the only sluggish one for the New York offense. Simms missed on a couple of throws, but observers felt they could have been caught. Another time, receiver Phil McConkey tripped, and the pass landed where McConkey would have been had he completed his route. So at halftime, it was still a 10-9 game, a game that could go either way in the 30 minutes of football that remained.

Simms was 12 of 15 in the first half, good for 102 yards. He was obviously having an outstanding day. But by contrast, Elway was 13 for 20, a lower percentage, yet he had thrown for 187 yards. Coupled with his scrambling, Elway had to be considered the more dynamic quarterback in the first half.

But then came quarter number three. That was when Simms and the Giants really began asserting themselves. On their first drive of the third period, they stalled with a fourth-and-one at their own 46. Coach Parcells sent punter Sean Landeta onto the field. But he also sent out reserve quarterback Jeff Rutledge. It was a fake punt, and Rutledge sneaked a yard for the first down.

Simms came back and went to work again. He hit Morris for 12, then threw to reserve running back Lee Rouson for 23. With the ball at the 17, he threw a perfect strike to tight end Mark Bavaro for a score. Raul Allegre's kick gave the Giants the lead at 16–10.

Later in the period, Simms drove the Giants downfield again. This time Allegre booted a 21-yard field goal to extend the lead to 19–10. The defense stopped the Broncos cold once more, and Simms immediately took advantage. This drive was highlighted by a flea flicker, a trick play where Simms gave the ball to halfback Morris. Morris faked a run, stopped suddenly and flipped the ball back to Simms. The QB then fired deep downfield to Phil McConkey, who caught it at the 20 and ran it all the way to the one. Morris scored on the following play and the kick made it a 26–10 game.

**Halfback Joe Morris flips the ball back to quarterback Simms (11) as the Giants begin a "flea flicker" play that netted a big gain in Super Bowl XXI.**

Simms still wasn't finished. With his great defense now putting a blanket over Elway, Phil was the main man. Quarterbacking with confidence and verve, he brought his club through the Denver defense again, culminating the drive with a six-yard TD toss to Mc-Conkey, who caught the ball after it deflected off the hands of Bavaro. The Giants and Simms were even getting the breaks on the bounces.

In the fourth period, Simms set up still another score with a nifty, 36-yard strike to Stacy Robinson. And when the final gun had sounded, the New York Giants had a one-sided 39–20 victory. They were Super Bowl champions at last.

As for Phil Simms, he had simply put on an incredible performance. Not only had he become a Super Bowl record breaker, but he was a unanimous choice as the game's Most Valuable Player. In the second half of the game alone, he had hit on all 10 of his passes for 166 yards. The 10 straight completions set a new record, as did his 88 percent completion accuracy, which he achieved with a 22 for 25 aerial act to break the old record of 73.5 percent, set by Cincinnati's Ken Anderson in the 1982 Super Bowl.

Was it vindication for a quarterback who had taken so much flak for so long? It had to be. He had put on perhaps the greatest show of any quarterback in Super Bowl history. His coach, Bill Parcells, called him "magnificent," adding, "He completed 22 of 25, and two of those three misses could have been caught. I don't think he threw a bad ball all day. For our team, he's the best guy I could have."

During the lean years, no one ever questioned Phil Simms' courage. Nor did they question his competitiveness. Just his ultimate ability. Now Simms has answered that last question. And he did it by becoming a record breaker, a record breaker in the one game where it meant the most—the Super Bowl.

# The Oldest Records in the Book

Over the years, there have been many records set, then broken, then broken again. Theoretically speaking, no record is safe, especially from the great players of today. Yet there are still some oldies but goodies, records that have stood the test of time. Let's take a closer look at some of these longest-standing NFL marks as well as the players who set them.

Whenever there is a football player who likes to get his uniform dirty, a blood-and-guts type who finishes a game with a torn jersey, a bloody nose, and a big smile on his face, somebody is there to call him a throwback. They say he's like the old timers, guys who played the game for the sheer joy of it, the pioneers who helped make the NFL what it is today.

Ernie Nevers wasn't a throwback. Oh, no. He was one of the players who helped invent the term, a hard-nosed fullback and defender who hated to come out of a game even for a minute. By the time he was a senior at Stanford University, he already had a reputation. In the Rose Bowl game that year (1924), Stanford lost to one of Knute Rockne's great Notre Dame teams. But the immortal Rockne was so impressed by Nevers that he called him a "fury in football boots."

Nevers was such a great athlete that he played major league baseball as well as pro football. He was a highly touted righthanded pitcher for the old St. Louis Browns beginning in 1926. The next year, 1927, while appearing in 27 games for the Brownies, Nevers gave up two home runs to Yankee immortal Babe Ruth, who was on his way to his magic number of 60 round trippers.

An injury, however, cut short Nevers' baseball career and he returned to the pro football wars full time. By 1929, he was a 26-year-old player-coach for the Chicago Cardinals. And coming into the Thanksgiving Day game against the crosstown rival Chicago Bears, Nevers was about to set a pair of records now listed as the oldest individual season or single game mark in the National Football League record book.

The game was played at Comiskey Park in Chicago on November 28, 1929. Neither team would win the NFL title that year, but the game was still for the City Championship, so emotions ran high. Only about 8,000 fans braved the bitter cold as the two teams took to an icy field. The opening minutes were scoreless, but then the Cardinals began moving the ball.

They drove downfield and Nevers went the final 10 yards for the first score. Ernie was also the team's

**11**

kicker, but his try for the extra point went wide. Then, before the quarter ended, the Cards were knocking on the door once more and it was Ernie Nevers who bulldozed in from the five-yard line for another tally. This time he made good on the kick and his club had a 13–0 lead. Midway through the second period, the big guy did it again, this time from six yards out. His kick made it a 20–0 game at the half.

The Bears had a star runner of their own in Red Grange, but as the second half began, Ernie Nevers had been the whole show. With their ground game going nowhere, the Bears tried the air route and connected on a long, 60-yard touchdown play to make it 20–6. But the Cards continued to play a bruising, ground-oriented game, and after driving down again, Nevers blasted over for his fourth score, this time from the one. His kick made it 27–6.

By now, the fans realized that their star fullback was putting on a show, and they began chanting for him to carry the football on every play. The big guy was psyched. He was giving everything he had and continuing to chew up the yardage.

Sure enough, early in the fourth period, he blasted over from close in for his fifth score of the day. And minutes later he rambled over the goal line from 10 yards out. His final extra point brought the score to 40–6. The Cardinals were City Champs and Ernie Nevers had put his name in the record books.

He had run for six touchdowns from the line of scrimmage, a mark that still stands today. In addition, he scored all of his team's points on the six TD's and the four extra points he booted. Those 40 points are still the most ever scored by one player in a single game.

Ernie Nevers went on to complete a Hall of Fame career. He was a player called the best ever at the time when there were the likes of Jim Thorpe and Red Grange also tearing up the gridiron. It was easy to predict that Nevers would go down as an all-time great. But what wasn't so easy to predict was the life of the great records he set on that cold November afternoon so long ago. They have stood the test of time as the oldest marks in the book.

Pro football's rushing record is a chapter in itself. The many great runners down through the years have challenged and set new marks time and again. No rushing record seems safe—especially in the era of longer seasons, bigger, stronger, faster athletes, improved training methods, and modern sports medicine.

But did you know that the first 1,000-yard rusher, and a man who held the single-season record for 13 years, also set a running mark that has stood for more than 50 years? It is now one of the oldest records in the NFL book.

The year was 1934 and the man Beattie Feathers, a fleet halfback with the Chicago Bears. Feathers didn't get to carry the call some three or four hundred times, the way modern runners often do. As a matter of fact, he carried the football only 101 times during the season. Today's runners would be complaining about a lack of work with that small number of carries. But, oh, what Beattie Feathers did when he had the pigskin.

He ran, cut, twisted, fought, sprinted, faked, followed his blockers, did it on his own—anything to make yardage. And when the smoke cleared, Beattie Feathers had gained 1,004 yards on those 101 carries. His total yardage was a record at the time, and it stood until Philadelphia's great Steve Van Buren ran for 1,008 yards in the 1947 season.

What, then, was so special about Feathers' achievement? Look at it this way. Van Buren was a great back. He's a Hall of Famer and considered by many as the first of the modern running backs. Yet it took him 217 carries to run for his 1,008 yards. Feathers ran for 1,004 on 101 carries!

And that's why Beattie Feathers is still in the record book. He averaged 9.94 yards a carry in 1934. It was an amazing number. Nearly 10 yards a pop in an era when defenses were geared to stop the run. But Beattie Feathers did it, and at the same time set a record that would still be standing a half century later.

Here's one that might surprise a lot of people. There was a punting record set way back in 1940 that still stands all these years later. With the improvements in all phases of the game, it is amazing that this mark has never been topped. Some may argue that today's punters often go for the "coffin corner" instead of all-out distance. But the booters back then did, too. And there were a lot of years and a lot of punters in between.

Who is this kicking specialist who set one of pro football's oldest records? He wasn't really a kicking specialist at all. He was Sammy Baugh, the man known as "Slingin'" Sam, one of the great quarterbacks of pro football's early days.

Baugh is a Hall of Famer, a tall Texan who starred for the Washington Redskins from 1937 to 1952. He was instrumental in making the forward pass a much more integral part of the pro game than it had ever been before. It's said that Baugh practiced his passing for hours on end, hanging an old tire on the end of a rope and tying the other end to a tree limb. He would then swing the tire back and forth and practice throwing the football through it from a variety of angles and distances.

The result was his passing excellence, and a number of championships for the Redskins. In fact, Slingin' Sam has one long-standing passing mark in the book. In a game against Boston on October 31, 1948, he attempted 24 passes and gained 446 yards. That comes out to an average gain per pass of 18.58 yards, still an NFL record for a single game.

But the oldest record still held by Sammy Baugh came from his foot, not his arm. Since there were no kicking specialists back then, one of the regular players handled the punting. Baugh loved to punt, and was particularly skilled at the quick kick, a maneuver rarely used today.

Since the Redskins used the old single wing formation where the quarterback took a direct snap from center, much as QB's do in the "shotgun" formation today, Baugh was always a threat to quick kick. In fact, during the 1942 championship game against the Chicago Bears, he got off a quick kick that turned the whole game around.

The Redskins had just brought the kickoff back to their own 12-yard line when Baugh entered the game. Strategies were different back then, and even though it was a first down play, Baugh decided to quick kick. His boot hit at the 50 and bounced all the way to the Chicago five-yard line. It went in the books as an 83-yard punt and it put the Bears in an early hole, just when they thought they had the Skins in a similar position.

So Sammy Baugh had a strong leg. In fact, he really showed it in the 1940 season. That year, he booted the ball 35 times, good for 1,799 yards. That averages out to 51.4 yards per kick, an all-time NFL record that serves to remind people that while records are made to be broken, some of them last a very long time.

# A Streak to Rival Joe D.'s

No, this is not an attempt to change horses in mid-stream. But, yes, the Joe D. is Joe DiMaggio the baseball player. And this is a book about football record breakers. But the comparison is valid. For Joe DiMaggio holds one of the greatest records in all of sports. He once hit safely in 56 consecutive ballgames. It's a mark that has stood for nearly 50 years, and there are many who feel it will stand forever.

Well, there is a similar record in football, and it was set by a player who enjoys the same stature that Di-Maggio has in his sport. The player is John Unitas, the legendary quarterback of the Baltimore Colts and a player considered by many as the greatest ever to play the position.

The record. Yes, like DiMaggio's, it is a streak, and a rather fantastic one. For John Unitas holds the NFL record for throwing at least one touchdown pass in 47 consecutive games. And that takes some doing. In many ways, Johnny U's standard is every bit the equal of DiMaggio's.

For one thing, a baseball season in DiMaggio's time was 154 games long. So Joe D. got in a fantastic groove back in 1941 and compiled his great record in about a two-month span. By contrast, the football season in Unitas' time was just 12 games long. Thus, Johnny U. needed all of three seasons and parts of two more to make his mark. In other words, he had to be in the touchdown groove every week for the better part of five seasons. One bad game during that period and it was over.

Most football fans, by now, know the rags to riches story of John Unitas. He started out as a quarterback nobody wanted. Coming out of the University of Louisville, he was unceremoniously cut by the Pittsburgh Steelers and left without a team. He could have called it quits right then and there. Instead, he began to call around, to see if anyone needed a quarterback.

Fortunately—for John Unitas, the city of Baltimore, and the pro football world at large—the Baltimore Colts answered his call. He was a walk-on who made the team as a backup signalcaller at the outset of the 1956 season. Injuries to the starting QB gave him his shot at playing by the end of the year. And in the final three games of that campaign, he managed to connect on TD passes each time. No one realized it then, but it was the beginning of a record.

By the next season, Unitas was a starter and the Colts were building an outstanding team. Johnny U. was surrounded by all the key elements a quarterback needed. Baltimore had a great offensive line to protect him from pass rushers. There were two great receivers in Raymond Berry and Lenny Moore, as well as a dependable tight end, Jim Mutscheller. Alan "The Horse" Ameche was the kind of fullback who kept defenses honest. In addition, the Colts had a tough, bruising defensive unit that made sure Unitas and the offense had the football a good deal of the time.

The Colts were a winning football team in 1957, and young John Unitas tossed at least one scoring pass in all 12 games. Most of the attention was focused on what a good quarterback he was becoming. At six feet one inch and 195 pounds, he wasn't big by today's standards. Nor did he have a real cannon for an arm. But he was a cool and supremely confident quarterback, one with instinct and vision, and a man who inspired his teammates to great achievements.

In 1958, the entire pro football world was to learn of John Unitas and the Colts. The club captured the NFL's Western Conference title and, in an incredible championship game, defeated the New York Giants 23–17 in sudden-death overtime, a game in which Unitas rallied his team from the brink of defeat.

Then came 1959, and football people began to notice the streak. He had missed a pair of games due to injury in '58, but as '59 started, his TD streak was at 25 consecutive games—already an NFL record. So the question now became: Just how far could John Unitas go?

The Colts repeated as Western Conference champs in '59, and once again whipped the Giants for their second straight NFL title. By this time, John Unitas was known as the best quarterback in football, and his touchdown streak had reached 37 consecutive games. He was well on his way to becoming a legend.

In 1960, the Colts fell off as a team. But John Unitas looked better than ever. He kept tossing touchdowns. In a game against Dallas on October 30, he threw for four scores, and a week later, against the tough Green Bay Packers, he fired for four more. Eight TD passes in two games. By the time the Colts faced the Detroit Lions on December 4, the streak had reached 46 games.

Early in the game against the Lions, the Colts were backed up at their own 20-yard line as Unitas dropped back to pass. He spotted Lenny Moore, his fleet half-back, going deep and fired. Moore gathered in the perfectly thrown aerial and outraced the defenders for an 80-yard score. It marked the forty-seventh straight game Unitas had thrown for a touchdown. Later, in the same game, Unitas and Moore hooked up on a 38-yard scoring pass. Little did anyone know then, the streak was about to end.

It happened the following week at the Los Angeles Coliseum, as the Colts visited the L.A. Rams. It was one of those rare days when the Colt offense just couldn't get on track. Unitas tried. He put the ball up 38 times, completing just 17 for 182 yards. He had one intercepted, but more important, he failed to connect for a touchdown. The Colts lost, 10–3, and one of sports' greatest streaks had come to an end.

During the 47-game streak, John Unitas had connected on 697 of 1,298 passes for 10,645 yards and 102 touchdowns. He was picked off just 61 times as the Colts won 31 of the 47 games as well as a pair of world championships. He would go on to set many more records in his great career, including becoming the first quarterback to throw for more than 40,000 career yards. And he played the game until he was 40 years old. No wonder he became a legend.

Many of John Unitas' records have since been broken by today's quarterbacks, who play in a much more pass-oriented environment. But in the more than a quarter of a century since Unitas connected with Lenny Moore for a TD pass in his 47th straight game, no quarterback has come close to approaching his record. The streak seems safe. Like DiMaggio's hitting streak in baseball, John Unitas' touchdown streak is a record that may never be broken.

# The Super Steelers

Pity poor Art Rooney. At the beginning of the decade of the 1970s, he may have been the most long-suffering man in sports. You see, Art Rooney was the longtime owner of the Pittsburgh Steelers, a beloved patriarch, respected by his peers, popular with his players and the fans. Why pity him? Because Art Rooney, a sports-man who loved the game of football, had seen his Steelers compete in the National Football League since 1933. And they had never won a title. In fact, the club had never even been in a championship game!

Hard to believe, but it was true. In four decades, the team had only come close a handful of times. There was an Eastern Division playoff with the Eagles in 1947. The Steelers lost, 21–0. Then there was 1963, when a season-ending victory over the New York Giants would have given Pittsburgh the divisional title. The Steelers were walloped, 33–16. But just when Art Rooney must have felt he was never going to win, things changed. And in the next decade, Art Rooney and the fans of Pittsburgh would not only see their team win, but they would see a record-setting decade that no one would ever forget.

To say the change began in 1969 would be a little difficult to believe at first. The Steelers finished that year with an abysmal 1–13 record, marking the third straight season they had been last in their division. In fact, the club's combined record for 1968 and 1969 was 3–24–1. How in the world could that be the beginning of something new?

For one thing, Art Rooney was tired of losing. Despite the long years of watching his team go down to defeat, he never got used to it.

"Losing is like a death in the family," he was known to say. And before 1969 he hired a new coach, a 37-year-old named Chuck Noll. Noll realized he had to completely rebuild the team, and he knew right away that he would begin with defense. His first draft choice that year was a mammoth defensive tackle from North Texas State, six-foot-four-inch, 270-pound "Mean" Joe Greene. The process had started.

Noll actually won his first game as Pittsburgh head coach in 1969, a 16–13 victory over Detroit. The problem was the team then went out and lost 13 straight games. But as Noll himself noted, "We weren't getting blown off the field."

During the next several years, Noll went about acquiring quality players. The names of some of the players joining the Steelers in those years now reads like a Who's Who of 1970's superstars. They were quarterback Terry Bradshaw, running-backs Franco Harris and Rocky Bleier, receivers Lynn Swann and John Stallworth, and a strong offensive line led by center Mike Webster and guard Jon Kolb. The defense was equally tough, with Green, L. C. Greenwood, Dwight White, Ernie Holmes on the line, Jack Ham, Jack Lambert, and Andy Russell at linebacker, and a strong secondary featuring the hard-hitting Mel Blount and Donnie Shell.

The club improved to 5–9 in 1970 and 6–8 in 1971. Still, it was hard to believe they were so close to the brink of greatness.

Tackle Joe Greene said, "Coach Noll and Dan Rooney [Art's son] had a plan to bring the Steelers out of the dark ages and they had the courage to stick with that plan. They decided to go for youth, for high-quality athletes with little experience, and then wait for them to mature."

In 1972, they matured. The Steelers surprised everyone by taking the American Conference Central Division title with an 11–3 season. It was the first title of any kind for the franchise in 40 years. But it was only step one. The club won its first playoff game that year with a dramatic, last-second victory over Oakland, 13–7, when Franco Harris caught a deflected pass and ran for a touchdown as time ran out.

But a week later the club lost a hard-fought game to eventual Super Bowl winner Miami, 21–17, a team that was to go through the year undefeated. So it was no disgrace. The next year the club was 10–4, the same as

Cincinnati, but the Bengals won the division because of a better conference record. Then Oakland whipped the Steelers in the first playoff game, 33–14. So they would have to wait still another year.

That was 1974, and the Steelers really came into their own. They won their division handily, posting a 10–3–1 record as the Steel Curtain defense yielded just 189 points in 14 games. In the playoffs, they whipped the high-scoring Buffalo Bills, 32–14, then went into the AFC title game against always tough Oakland.

The game was close for three periods, the Raiders taking a 10–3 lead into the final session. But quarterback Bradshaw rallied the offense for three scores and the Steelers won, 24–13. After 42 years, they had won a championship and now were going to the Super Bowl.

In Super Bowl IX, Pittsburgh met the Minnesota Vikings, a club led by scrambling quarterback Fran Tarkenton, versatile halfback Chuck Foreman, and a defense equal to that of the Steelers. It was a tightly played game all the way.

After a scoreless first period, the Steelers got on the board when Dwight White downed Tarkenton in the end zone for a safety. The half ended with a baseball-like score, 2–0. Then in the third period the Steelers recovered a fumble of the opening kickoff at the Viking 30-yard line. After three running plays, Franco Harris had taken it in. The kick made it 9–0.

Minnesota's only score came in the fourth period on a blocked punt that was recovered in the end zone. The extra point was missed, but it was still a game at 9–6.

A host of Steel Curtain defenders stop Minnesota's Dave Osborn in Super Bowl IX. Defense played a major role in all four Steeler Super Bowl triumphs.

Then Bradshaw engineered a methodical, seven-minute drive. From the four, the QB hit his tight end, Larry Brown, for the last score of the game. It ended at 16–6, and the Steelers were world champions—at last!

The football world couldn't have been happier for Art Rooney. He had waited so long. Co-captain Andy Russell presented the longtime owner with the game ball, proclaiming, "This one's for The Chief. It's been a long time coming."

It sure was. But other teams have won Super Bowl games before. Where's the record? Franco Harris had set one by gaining 158 yards rushing. But what about the Steelers? They had won a hard-fought victory, but it wasn't really a great football game.

Jump to 1975. The Steelers were back, going 12–2 in the regular season and looking like pro football's best team. In the playoffs, they clobbered Baltimore, 28–10, then whipped Oakland, 16–10, for another AFC crown. So it was back to the Super Bowl. Only this time their opponents were the Dallas Cowboys, an explosive team led by clutch quarterback Roger Staubach.

This game belonged to Lynn Swann. The acrobatic wide receiver came out of a hospital bed after receiving a concussion in the Oakland game and put on one of the great performances in Super Bowl history. He caught just four passes, but they were good for 161 yards and the MVP prize as the Steelers won it, 21–17.

Swann's catches covered 32, 53, 12, and 64 yards. But they weren't ordinary grabs. As one writer put it: "The first catch was incredible, the second unbelievable, the third was merely a standard, difficult professional reception. The fourth was a blazing touchdown that earned Swann 'Most Valuable Player' honors."

So this time the Steelers won in spectacular fashion—two Super Bowls in a row. But that, too, had been done before. The Green Bay Packers had won the first two Super Bowl games, and the Miami Dolphins had done it right before the Steelers. So where's the record? Three in a row. No team had done that before.

For a while, it looked as if the Steelers would be the first. They won their divisional title in 1976 with a 10–4 record. During the season, both Franco Harris and Rocky Bleier rushed for over 1,000 yards, but by the time the club faced Oakland for the AFC title, both runners were hurt and on the sidelines. The offense bogged down and Oakland won, 24–7.

Then in 1977, the club had more injuries that resulted in a defensive breakdown. The Steel Curtain had yielded just 138 points during 14 games in 1976. Yet in '77 they gave up 243. The club won the A.F.C. Central title with a 9–5 mark, but lost in the first playoff game to Denver, 34–21. Was the era of the Steelers coming to an end?

Hardly. The club rebounded with a vengeance in '78, posting a 14–2 mark in the first year of the 16-game schedule. The defense also rebounded, giving up just 195 points, best in the league. It looked as if the club was ready for another run at the Super Bowl.

This time they looked like a steamroller. First they whipped Denver, 33–10. Then, on a wet and slick field at Three Rivers Stadium in Pittsburgh, the Steelers buried the Houston Oilers, 34–5, to win the AFC title once again. Terry Bradshaw and company exploded for 17 points in the final 48 seconds of the first half to take a 31–3 lead into the locker room. In the second half, the weather was so bad that neither team could mount much offense.

But it was off to the Super Bowl for a third time, and waiting for the Steelers again were the defending champs, the Dallas Cowboys. This one would be truly memorable and would finally serve to stamp the Steeler team as one of the greatest ever.

It was like two giants going at each other. Both bent, but neither broke. It was almost a battle of wills, to see which of the teams would have that last bit of mental toughness to prevail. Pittsburgh scored first when Bradshaw hit Stallworth from 28 yards out. Next it was Dallas' turn, as Staubach found Tony Hill from the 39. The game was a 7–7 deadlock after one quarter.

The Cowboys grabbed the lead in the second when linebacker Mike Hegman returned a fumble 37 yards for a score. Bradshaw came right back. He hit Stallworth on a long, 75-yard TD strike to tie it again. Then, before the half, he drove his club downfield and threw seven yards to Rocky Bleier for still another score. At the half, the Steelers led it, 21–14.

A third-quarter Dallas field goal made it 21–17, but in the fourth, the Steelers seemed to sew it up. First Franco Harris scored on a bruising, 22-yard run. Then Bradshaw went back to work and connected with Swann on an 18-yard scoring pass. That made it 35–17 with just over six minutes left. Many of the Steelers were already celebrating.

"That made me mad," said quarterback Bradshaw. "I remembered the Super Bowl three years earlier when Dallas came back and threatened to pull it out."

With a quarterback like Roger Staubach, anything

was possible. He came out on the field after the Pittsburgh kickoff and promptly drove his team 89 yards in eight plays, throwing a seven-yard TD strike to Billy Joe Dupree. It was now 35–24, with 2:27 remaining. Dallas then tried an onsides kick, and when it was bobbled by the Steelers, the Cowboys got the ball back at their own 48.

Once more Staubach went to work. He threw eight straight passes, racking up another TD when he hit Butch Johnson from four yards out. The extra point had made it 35–31, with just 22 seconds remaining. If Dallas could recover another onsides kick . . . well.

To no one's surprise, they tried it. But this time Rocky Bleier fell on the ball and the Steelers were able to run out the clock. They had done it—won a record-setting third Super Bowl. Bradshaw was the MVP with a 318-yard, four-touchdown performance. Art Rooney's team now had the stamp of greatness upon it, no doubt.

But the club wasn't ready to call it quits. They were the team of the '70s, just as the Green Bay Packers had been the team of the '60s. So they wanted to close out the decade in style. They finished the 1979 season at 12–4, winning yet another AFC Central crown. Then they trounced Miami, 34–14, in the divisional play-off, and won the AFC title by beating Houston, 27–13. Now it was back to the Super Bowl for a fourth time, with their opponents the surprising Los Angeles Rams.

This one was just icing on the cake. With the same veteran cast of characters that had been in the three previous Super Bowl victories, the Steelers went to work. It wasn't easy. Very few are. The Rams, in fact, played Pittsburgh tough for three quarters, leading 7–3 after one, 13–10 at the half, and 19–17 after three.

But as the old expression goes, "When the going gets tough, the tough get going." And if there was a tough, gritty team in the '70s, it was the Pittsburgh

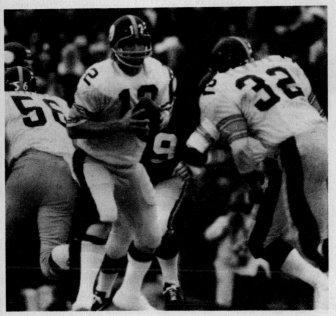

**Pittsburgh Steeler quarterback Terry Bradshaw gives the ball to his fullback, Franco Harris. It was a scene repeated many times as the Steelers rolled to a record-setting four Super Bowl victories in the 1970s.**

Steelers. Quarterback Bradshaw had already thrown three interceptions and he was mad. Early in the fourth quarter, the Steelers had a third down and eight on their own 27. They decided to go for broke.

"It was a play we practiced all week," said wide receiver John Stallworth, "and it hadn't worked once."

Nevertheless, Bradshaw took the snap and dropped back. Stallworth sprinted downfield 15 yards, then hooked in as if he was going over the middle. When the defenders took the fake, Stallworth went deep and Bradshaw released the ball. The speedy receiver gathered in the perfectly thrown aerial at the Los Angeles 34 and raced all the way to the end zone to complete a big, 73-yard touchdown play.

The Steelers went wild. Roy Gerela's kick made it a 24–19 game. But the Rams wouldn't quit. They drove all the way to the Pittsburgh 32. Quarterback Vince Ferragamo then tried a pass which was picked off by linebacker Jack Lambert at the 16.

Then, with just 5:24 left, the Steelers were at their own 30 and Bradshaw went to Stallworth again. Same play. Another long gainer, this one for 45 yards to the Rams' 25. Two plays later, Bradshaw threw toward Jim Smith in the end zone. The ball fell untouched, but an interference call against the Rams put it on the one-yard line. Three more plays and Franco Harris smashed over for the insurance touchdown.

The final was 31–19. The Steelers had done it again. Four Super Bowls—four victories—a record unmatched since the super game began back in 1967.

"I was never so happy to see a game end," said Terry Bradshaw, who was once again the MVP. "There was so much more pressure than in the previous Super Bowls."

Pressure, yes. But the Steelers handled it as they had each of the other times. Whenever there was trouble, someone was ready to pick up the slack. If it wasn't Bradshaw or Harris, it was Swann or Stallworth. If it wasn't Greene or Lambert, it was Jack Ham or Mel Blount. Great teams have great players who do that for you.

For Art Rooney, it was the perfect end to an incredible decade. He had waited more than 40 years for a championship. Now he had four of them, all in the biggest spectacle of them all, the Super Bowl. It was surely a record to make him proud.

"This might be the greatest team of all time," he said after the big win.

Greatest ever? Comparisons are hard to make. Greatest team of its era? Definitely. A deep, balanced team that rose to the occasion when all the chips were on the table. The result? A record-setting performance that may never be matched.

# The Team that Couldn't Win

Expansion. That's been a big word in all professional sports during the past 25 years. Football, baseball, basketball, and hockey have all added new teams and new cities, expanding their leagues and their schedules. It's not easy for an expansion team, however. Despite enthusiastic fans happy to see a professional team in their city, and owners anxious to build a winner, expansion teams usually have their troubles for the first few years.

That's the way it has to be. After all, expansion teams don't have stars. They have a combination of aging veterans, castoffs getting another chance, and youngsters lacking in experience. It's not the best of circumstances for winning ballgames.

A look at some of the expansion teams since 1960 shows a similar consistent futility. The Dallas Cowboys were 0–11–1 in their initial season of 1960. They might not have won a single game, but at least they salvaged a tie, a 31–31 deadlock with the New York Giants. It couldn't have made the Giants too happy. But a year later, Tom Landry's new team won four games. By 1965, they reached .500, and a year later took their first divisional title.

In 1961, the Minnesota Vikings joined the NFL. They started a rookie quarterback named Fran Tarkenton who dazzled opponents with his daring scrambling. The Vikes actually won three games their first season, finishing at 3–11. Three years later, the Vikings were at 8–5–1, and by 1968 they had taken a division crown. Both the Cowboys and Vikings grew quickly.

The Miami Dolphins joined the American Football League in 1966 and won three games. They won four the next year, and by 1970 they were good enough to finish at 10–4 and make the playoff. Two years after that, they won the Super Bowl and had a 17–0 record for the season. They had done that in just seven years.

Other expansion teams haven't developed that quickly, but they've always managed to win a few games in those early years. The Atlanta Falcons joined the league in 1966 and won three times, though the following season they won only once, then twice the year after that. In their fourth year, they won six games.

The New Orleans Saints came in the year after the Falcons, in 1967. They, too, won three times in their initial season, four times the next year, and took five victories the year after that. The Cincinnati Bengals also won three games their first year in the league. That seemed to be a magic number.

But then there were the Tampa Bay Buccaneers. The Bucs joined the AFC in 1976, gathering the usual collection of players and selecting John McKay, a highly successful college coach at the University of Southern California (USC), to lead them. Would they, too, win three games their first season?

It didn't work out that way. In fact, the Bucs didn't even win two games. Nor did they win one—not a single victory. And unlike the winless 1960 Cowboys, they didn't even have a tie. The 1976 Tampa Bay Buccaneers lost all 14 of their games. And they lost many of them big. The Raiders beat them, 49–16; the Colts, 42–17; the Broncos, 48–13; the Browns, 24–7; the Bengals, 21–0; the Steelers, 42–0; the Chargers, 23–0; the Jets, 34–0; and the Oilers, 20–0. Not much to cheer about.

There were a few close ones. The Chiefs beat the Bucs, 28–19; the Bills just squeaked by, 14–9; and in perhaps the biggest game of the year against interstate rival Miami, the Bucs were just nosed out, 23–20. But they lost all 14, and they hoped to make up some ground in 1977.

The club had tried to build its defense first, making Oklahoma tackle Lee Roy Selmon its top draft choice in 1976. The next year they took Southern Cal's great running back, Ricky Bell. It sure seemed like the time had come to log some wins, especially after the club won a pair of preseason games, beating Green Bay and Baltimore.

But once the regular season started, it was more of the same. They opened with a 13–3 loss to Philadelphia, then were beaten by the Vikings, 9–3. The defense seemed to be competitive, but the offense was still lacking. So the club continued to lose. Washington shut them out. So did Green Bay. The Rams also blanked them. Everyone was hungry for a victory, but the losing streak was over 20 games and still going.

Toward the end of the year, Coach McKay tried to soften the disappointment. "With consistency at quarterback and healthy tight ends, I believe we could have won three to six games this year," he proclaimed. "The way our defense has played, 14 points would have been enough to win a lot of games for us."

Maybe he was right. On December 11, the Bucs came into the Louisiana Superdome to meet the New Orleans Saints. And they were in the record books. After losing all 14 games in 1976, they had come right back to drop the first 12 games of 1977. That made 26 consecutive losses, by far the longest losing streak in NFL history. The previous mark had been 19. The question was, when would it end?

It would seem that when the Bucs finally won, they'd just eke one out by a low score, something like 10–7 or 14–13. But at the Superdome on that December day, the Bucs suddenly played like a Super Bowl Team. They intercepted three Saints passes and turned each one into a touchdown. When the smoke cleared, the team had its first win ever—a big 33–14 victory.

There was a festive atmosphere in Tampa all week. And when the Bucs hosted the St. Louis Cardinals in the season finale, they surprised everyone by pulling off a 17–7 upset. So, after running their record-breaking losing streak to 26 games, the Bucs won two games in a row, which to their fans must have seemed like a miracle.

The Bucs have continued to be an up-and-down franchise. In their third season, they won five games, and the next year, 1979, they surprised the football world by winning the NFC Central Division title with a 10–6 mark. Then they shocked the experts again by defeating Philadelphia in the division playoffs, 24–17. The four-year-old franchise was now one game away from going to the Super Bowl. That would have been another record in itself.

Unfortunately, the Rams ended the Bucs' hopes with a 9–0 victory in the NFC title game. But just getting there was miraculous, especially to those who witnessed the team's first 26 games.

# Marino's Touchdown Magic

They called them the Class of '83. Never before in recent memory had so many outstanding college quarterbacks been available in the pro draft at the same time. There was surely going to be a scramble for the talents of John Elway of Stanford, Jim Kelly of Miami, Tony Eason of Illinois, Todd Blackledge of Penn State, Ken O'Brien of Cal-Davis, and Dan Marino of Pittsburgh.

All the QB's were given a chance to become big stars in the National Football League, and since that draft each has made his mark in the pros. But, strangely enough, the one who has gone on to set a number of great records was the last of the six taken in the first round that season.

John Elway was all-everything that year. He was being hailed as the next super quarterback in the NFL. Jim Kelly was also highly rated, though he was recovering from a shoulder injury. Blackledge had just led Penn State to a National Championship, while Eason was steady as a rock at Illinois. O'Brien was a sleeper, having attended a less prominent college than the others, but reports on him were all glowing. Then there was Dan Marino of Pittsburgh.

A year earlier, Dan Marino would have been ranked right up there with the best of them. He had been outstanding as a sophomore and a junior. But his senior year was something less than great. The stats were down; the team wasn't as strong.

On draft day, Marino sat and watched the other signalcallers being tabbed. Elway was the first choice of the entire league; Baltimore grabbed him (and later traded him to Denver). Buffalo picked Kelly (who went to the United States Football League, where he was a record setter before returning to Buffalo in 1986). Eason went to New England, Blackledge to Kansas City, and O'Brien to the New York Jets. All those teams passed on Dan Marino.

Which is not to say that Marino's luck was all bad. Because the later in the first round the better the team that is choosing. And Marino was picked by a good one, all right. The Miami Dolphins made him their number one draft choice.

The Dolphins, coached by the dynamic Don Shula, were among the NFL's elite, having already appeared in four Super Bowls, winning two of them. They had won the AFC's Eastern Division title in 1981, then finished 7–2 in the strike-shortened season of '82, winning three playoff games in the special tournament that year before losing in the Super Bowl to Washington.

So Dan Marino was joining a solid team capable of going all the way in any season. Coach Shula always saw to that. The question was: How would he use Marino in his rookie year? The Dolphins had a solid veteran in Don Strock, but he never had a real shot as a regular. And it wasn't long, as his playing time increased, before Dan Marino was impressing everyone who saw him. Sure enough, by the second half of the 1983 season, Dan Marino was the Dolphins' top signal-caller.

That wasn't all. Not only was he starting, but Dan Marino was *starring*, playing like a seasoned pro. At six feet four inches, 215 pounds, Marino was showing poise, strength, good vision, a quick release, and a shotgun for an arm. With receivers like Mark Duper, Mark Clayton, Nat Moore, and Tony Nathan, Marino had the targets, and he was hitting them.

The Dolphins finished the season with a 12–4 mark, and another divisional title. And though they were upset in the first round of the playoffs by Seattle, Dan Marino had established himself. He even wound up the AFC's leading passer by completing 173 of 296 passes for 2,210 yards and 20 touchdowns. He completed 58.4 percent of his passes and was intercepted only six times. But as good as he was, no one was prepared for what Dan Marino was about to accomplish in 1984.

With the Dolphin offense now geared for his considerable talents, he went to work. In the opening game against Washington, the big guy completed 21 of 28 passes for 311 yards and five touchdowns. Yes, five!

**Miami's record-breaking quarterback, Dan Marino, stands tall as always as he gets set to pass against the L.A. Raiders.**

But he didn't stop there. The next week he threw for two scores, then three, then two more. Against St. Louis a week later, he had a 429-yard game and three more scores. He seemed almost unstoppable.

Some of the other quarterbacks from the Class of '83 were beginning to show their stuff, but none was as advanced as Dan Marino. He was already looking as good as any veteran quarterback in the game. And the Miami passing attack had defenses all around the league scrambling for a way to stop it.

Not only did Marino have the football world at large talking about his performance, but he had his team winning big. They were a lock to take the AFC Eastern title once again. And Dan Marino, besides emerging as a team leader, was also looking to make a run at several NFL passing records.

The way he was throwing the football, it began to look as if he'd have a shot at the single season record for attempts, completions, and yards. San Diego's Dan Fouts had thrown an amazing 609 passes in 1981 and completed 360 of them, both league records. He also set a yardage mark that same year with 4,802.

Still another record that seemed within reach was the 36 touchdown passes thrown by George Blanda of Houston in 1961, and tied by the Giants' Y. A. Tittle in 1963. So that one went back a long way. It was almost inconceivable that a second year quarterback could be challenging these kinds of records. After all, it was always said that it takes at least four or five years to make a good professional quarterback, no matter how great the man was in college.

None of that seemed to matter to Dan Marino. Week after week, he just kept firing. After 12 games, he had thrown for 32 scores. With four games still remaining, he seemed a cinch to set a new record. But the young quarterback was about to show that nothing rattled him, not the swarming defenses out to stop him, and not the pressure of approaching long-standing records.

Against the New York Jets, Marino completed 19 of 31 passes, good for 192 yards. That was to be the only game of the year in which he threw for less than 200 yards. But with those 192 yards came four more touchdowns, enabling him to tie the record set by Blanda and Tittle.

A week later, against the always tough Los Angeles Raiders, Marino really went to work. He put the ball in the air 57 times, completing 35 for a huge 470 yards . . . and another four touchdowns! He had set a new NFL record with 40 touchdown passes. And still he wasn't finished. He was 29 of 41 for 404 yards against the Colts. And guess what else? Another four scores. Now he had 44 TD passes with one week remaining.

Not one to waste time, Marino faced the Dallas Cowboys the same way he had faced every other team in 1984. He put the ball in the air with supreme confidence. When it was over, Marino had completed 23 of 40 passes for 340 yards. And for the fourth consecutive week, he had thrown for a total of four touchdowns. He had not only broken the old record of 36, he had totally wiped it out!

That wasn't all. His brilliant quarterbacking helped the Dolphins to a 14–2 record, second best in the NFL to San Francisco's 15–1. In addition, he had also produced a number of additional records. For the season, he had completed 362 of 564 passes for 5,084 yards and a completion percentage of 64.2. With his 48 touchdown passes went a scant 17 interceptions.

While his 564 attempts didn't break Dan Fouts' record, his 362 completions set a new standard. And along the way he became the first quarterback in NFL history to throw for more than 5,000 yards in a single season, as well as the first to compile four 400-yard games during the season. He was truly incredible.

It seemed that no matter what Dan Marino did in 1984 he came away with a record. In the AFC title game against Pittsburgh, he led the Dolphins to a 45–28 triumph by setting a championship game mark of 421 yards (completing 21 of 32) through the air and with four touchdown tosses.

And even when the Dolphins came up short, as they did in the Super Bowl that year, Marino was putting his name in the books. A red-hot San Francisco team took apart the Miami defense and forced Dan to play from behind. The Niners won the game impressively, 38–16, while Marino set Super Bowl marks with 29 completions and 50 attempts. Unfortunately, he was forced to throw so much because he was playing catch-up. Like all the great ones, he didn't make excuses.

"They played us the best any team has played against us defensively," he said. "They took us out of our scheme. We knew we had to throw the ball against a four-man line—and we didn't."

Though the defeat was difficult to take, it didn't take the luster off Dan Marino's achievements. And it didn't make him any less confident when throwing the football. In 1985, he led the Dolphins to another divisional title and finished the season as one of the top passers in the league, with 336 completions in 567 tries for 4,137 yards and 30 touchdowns.

And the following year, 1986, with the Dolphin defense breaking down, Marino had to pass even more. Though the club didn't make the playoffs, Dan Marino's arm made them a dangerous opponent all year, and once again got the quarterback into the record book.

In 1986, Dan Marino set a new record with 623 pass attempts and he broke his own mark with 378 completions. His passing gained 4,746 yards and he threw for 44 touchdowns, approaching his own standard of two years earlier. And he had done all this in just four short seasons.

The Class of '83—six quarterbacks who were taken in the first round—hasn't disappointed. Though still somewhat inconsistent, John Elway took the Denver Broncos all the way to the Super Bowl in 1986. Tony Eason has been troubled by injuries, but he helped get New England to the Super Bowl in '85. Jim Kelly hung up some amazing numbers in the USFL and shows signs of doing the same thing with Buffalo. Ken O'Brien led the entire NFL in passing in 1985 and was doing the same thing in '86 before a late-season slump slowed him down. Todd Blackledge has battled his way into the starting lineup at Kansas City.

But Dan Marino is the record setter. Perhaps no quarterback in the history of the game has put his name in the books so often in such a short time. And if the past is any indication, there is still a whole lot more to come.

# More Aerial Magic

To be a record breaker, you've got to be good. But in many cases, you've also got to be lucky. When quarterback Dan Fouts came out of the University of Oregon in 1972, he might have been drafted by a conservative team, one that liked to keep the ball on the ground and throw only when necessary. If that had happened, Dan Fouts might not have been a record breaker.

As it was, Dan spent several seasons with the San Diego Chargers hanging up mediocre numbers. He found himself battling with other quarterbacks for playing time, was hurt on a number of occasions, and once even held out part of the season looking for a better contract. After five seasons in San Diego, Dan Fouts was still not considered one of the premier quarterbacks in the National Football League.

Then, midway into the 1978 season, the Chargers got a new coach, and it changed Dan Fouts' whole career. That's what is meant by luck. Don Coryell was the coach and his philosophy was to throw the football.

When the new coach had time to put in his system, and find the personnel to go with it, "Air Coryell" was born. And the triggerman was Dan Fouts.

"The attitude of the coach is very important," Dan once said. "He has to want to pass, then teach it properly and be willing to work on it by the hour. As far as I'm concerned, passing is the best way to win football games, because it's the only way you can average nine or ten yards a play. . . . As a pro quarterback I've found out that most coaches would rather run. That's why I have so much respect for Don Coryell."

By 1979, Air Coryell was in full bloom. Dan was throwing to wide receivers like John Jefferson and Charlie Joiner, and a big rookie tight end named Kellen Winslow. It didn't take long. By the end of the season, Dan Fouts was a record breaker.

Dan had completed 332 of 530 passes, good for a record-breaking 4,082 yards. His completion percentage was 62.6, and he threw for 24 touchdowns. It was just the beginning. A year later, Dan threw for 4,715 yards, breaking his own record, and a year after that, in 1981, he cracked it again with 4,802 passing yards. He was also setting new marks for completions with 348 in 1980 and 360 the next year. In 1981, he set still another mark with 609 pass attempts.

That wasn't all. In 1980, he had thrown for 300 or more yards in eight different games, still another record-breaking performance. There was little doubt that Air Coryell and Dan Fouts set a trend that continued into the mid-1980s. More teams were throwing the ball,

The triggerman for "Air Coryell," San Diego's Dan Fouts gets ready to throw in heavy traffic. Running the first of the so-called passing offenses, Fouts became a multi–record breaker.

and more offenses were built around strong-armed young quarterbacks willing to put the ball in the air time and again.

That's why records are made to be broken. Since 1981, Dan Fouts has continued as a top-flight quarterback. But his records have largely been eclipsed, most of them by Miami's Dan Marino, who has set new standards for attempts, completions, yardage, and 300-yard games in a season.

But Dan Fouts isn't finished. There is one great record that he still holds which shows that he was the pioneer of the sustained passing attack. Through the 1986 season, Dan Fouts had thrown for 300 yards or more in a game 48 times. His nearest rival is John Unitas, who did it a mere 26 times.

Dan also has a chance at some other all time marks. He has moved into second place on the all time yardage list, becoming the third quarterback in history to throw for more than 40,000 yards in a career. Fran Tarkenton is the leader with just over 47,000. Dan is also the second quarterback, besides Tarkenton, to complete more than 3,000 passes.

So Dan Fouts' record-breaking days may not be over. He's been a tough leader, a competitor, a quarterback with outstanding downfield vision and a quick arm. Add some luck, the right situation, and it adds up to success.

Here's a great trivia question for experts on record breakers. What two Hall-of-Fame quarterbacks became record breakers in different games on the same day? (Now for a couple of clues. One of the QB's broke a record held by the other, while the second signalcaller set a mark that will never be broken due to the changing nature of the game.)

Time's up. The answers are Sid Luckman and Sammy Baugh, the two top quarterbacks of their time and strong rivals throughout the 1940s. Luckman played for George Halas and the Chicago Bears and is credited with being the first T-formation quarterback. Slingin' Sammy Baugh was a tremendous passer, the forerunner of the great quarterbacks of today.

The two QB's had faced each other many times, often hooking up in memorable games, not to mention title contests. In his rookie year of 1937, Baugh passed his Washington Redskins to a 28–21 victory over the Bears. Luckman wasn't the Chicago quarterback that day, but he was three years later, in 1940, when the Bears whipped the Redskins in the most one-sided title game ever, 73–0.

Two years later, Baugh and the Skins got revenge, whipping the Bears for the title, 14–6. But a year after that it was Chicago's turn. Luckman set a record by throwing five TD passes in a title game as the Bears beat the Redskins, 41–21. So it's obvious what great rivals these two quarterbacks were.

But the records mentioned earlier were not set in the same game. They happened on November 14, 1943. Luckman and the Bears were playing the New York Giants in New York, Luckman's home town. Some of the fans there decided to hold a Sid Luckman Day. Well, their hero didn't disappoint them.

Shortly after the opening kickoff, Luckman went to the air and fired a touchdown pass to Jim Benton. Things settled down until late in the second quarter when the Bear QB found Cornelius Berry for another TD toss. After intermission, Luckman went back to work and hit Hampton Pool for a score. A short time later he went upstairs for 33 yards to Harry Clark for his fourth touchdown pass of the day.

The record at the time was six, held by . . . you guessed it, Sammy Baugh. Could Luckman match Baugh? He was sure trying. He threw his fifth scoring aerial to Jim Benton, then a sixth to George Wilson. He had tied Baugh's record, and with some time still left on the clock, everyone began rooting for him to break it.

Finally, in the closing seconds of the game, Sid Luckman went deep to Hampton Pool. The receiver caught the ball on his fingertips as he crossed the goal line, holding it just long enough for the score to count. Seven touchdown passes! A new record, one that has since been tied by a number of players, but never broken. And Sid Luckman was the first to do it. Oh yes, the final score of the game was 56–7.

While Sid Luckman was in the process of breaking Sammy Baugh's record, the Washington quarterback was at home as the Redskins hosted the Detroit Lions. The Redskins won big that day, whipping the Lions, 42–20. While Sammy Baugh didn't throw seven touchdown passes, he was very instrumental in the Redskins' victory. In fact, along the way he set a record that will undoubtedly never be broken.

You see, it was still the era of two-way football. So while Sammy Baugh was the Redskins' regular quarterback, he was also a regular defensive back, a 60-minute man. And on this day, he showed the same kind of outstanding skills at both positions.

From his quarterback slot, he led the Skins' offense by firing four touchdown passes. It wasn't seven as Luckman had thrown, but it was a good day's work nonetheless. That leaves just one problem. Where's the record? Well, the other half of it came on defense. When he wasn't throwing his four touchdown passes, Sammy Baugh was busy at the other end, intercepting four passes!

That was the record. He became the only man in NFL history to throw four TD passes and intercept four passes in the same game. And because quarterbacks no longer play defense, it's a record you can safely say will stand forever.

There's little doubt that today's quarterbacks throw the ball more often than at any other time in NFL history. All you have to do is look at the stats compiled by the likes of Dan Fouts, Dan Marino, Phil Simms, and John Elway. These guys can air it out. But so could the quarterbacks in the old days. They just didn't do it quite so often.

Slingin' Sammy Baugh, for instance, put the ball up

354 times back in 1947 and threw for 2,938. There's little doubt that the tall Texan would have even bigger stats if he played today. Another great quarterback of that era, Norm Van Brocklin, also loved to hang the ball out. He did it for both the Los Angeles Rams and Philadelphia Eagles in his career. And he left behind one record that continues to stand.

Van Brocklin came up with the Rams in 1949. L.A. already had a topnotch quarterback in Bob Waterfield, but Van Brocklin was so good that the Rams found playing time for both signalcallers. In fact, a look at the NFL record book shows that Van Brocklin was the league's leading passer in 1950. The next year Waterfield held the honor, and the year after that Van Brocklin was back on top. So the Rams had a two-pronged passing attack that saw them in the NFL title game three straight years from 1949 to 1951.

It was the first game of the 1951 season when Van Brocklin got himself into the record books with an incredible performance. The Rams were playing the old New York Yanks at the Los Angeles Coliseum and the "Dutchman," as Van Brocklin was called, had the hot hand. He began throwing early and often, showing the kind of offense you would see today. And it paid big dividends.

Blessed with two all-pro receivers, Tom Fears and Elroy "Crazylegs" Hirsch, Van Brocklin had the targets. And on this day, Elroy Hirsch was as hot as his quarterback. He caught four Van Brocklin tosses for touchdowns, covering 46, 47, 26, and one yard. The

Dutchman also connected with halfback Verda "Vitamin A" Smith on a long, 67-yard pass play for another score. When the game ended, the Rams had a 54–14 victory, and the Dutchman was the talk of the town.

Van Brocklin had completed 27 of 41 passes. Five of his completions had gone for touchdowns. But the big story was his yardage. Those 27 completions were good for an amazing 554 yards! It was the most yards any quarterback had ever accumulated via the air lanes in a single game. And it still is! Nearly 40 years after setting the mark, Van Brocklin still holds the record. It's a worthy target for today's strong-armed quarterbacks. And a tough one, too.

Of course, there are also some passing records in the book that today's quarterbacks hope will stay there. In other words, they don't want to break them. One of those happened at Comiskey Park in Chicago on September 24, 1950. The Chicago Cardinals were playing their season opener against the Philadelphia Eagles.

Chicago quarterback Jim Hardy wanted to get his season off to a good start. And when his team fell behind early, Hardy went to the air, maybe a little more than he really wanted. Because things began going sour and Hardy just couldn't seem to make it right. Yet he kept throwing.

Jim Hardy put the ball up 39 times that late September afternoon. He completed just 12 of his passes—that is, to his own teammates. There were another eight passes he completed. Only they were to Philadelphia defenders! That's right. Jim Hardy set an NFL record by throwing eight interceptions in a single game. Needless to say, his team lost, 45–7.

A couple of strange twists. Two Eagle players picked off seven of the eight passes. Russ Craft got four of them, while Joe Sutton pilfered three. Hardy should have kept the ball away from them.

Then, a week later, Jim Hardy got even. Playing against the Baltimore Colts, the Cardinals were trailing, 13–7, at the half. Fortunately, Jim Hardy wasn't gun-shy because of the eight intercepts the week before. He went back up top and rallied his team to a 55–13 victory. And he did it by throwing for six touchdowns, one short of the record. Receiver Bob Shaw was on the catching end of five of Hardy's TD aerials. That put Shaw's name in the record book, and it's stayed there, the mark being tied once by San Diego's Kellen Winslow in 1981.

On the other side of the Jim Hardy coin, there is Bart Starr. Starr was the meticulous quarterback of the Green Bay Packers during their dynasty years under Vince Lombardi. Starr wasn't blessed with a great arm like many of the other quarterbacks, but he was smart and resourceful, and he played within his limitations. That means he didn't make many mistakes. He was also a clutch quarterback who was particularly dangerous on key third-down situations.

Never was that more in evidence than in the first ever Super Bowl, when Starr and his Packer teammates were going up against the Kansas City Chiefs. The

Packers won the game, 35–10. Starr was his usual accurate self, completing 16 of 23 passes, and on third-down plays he led his club to first downs 10 of 13 times. That's outstanding.

However, Starr was intercepted once in Super Bowl I. It marked the first time in 174 pass attempts that one of his aerials was picked off. Not bad, you say. A lot better than Jim Hardy's eight interceptions in one game. That's for sure. But it wasn't Bart Starr's best. For that, turn to the 1964 and 1965 seasons.

That's when Starr compiled a great record. He threw a total of 294 passes without having one grabbed by an opposing player. That's a lesson in accuracy that any quarterback would admire. And it's a record that will be very hard to beat.

# Running to Daylight . . .
## and to Records

This may be the most glamorous one of them all. Whenever a running back is going after a great record, the whole football world seems to focus upon it. There is something very special about being one of the premier running backs in the National Football League. And one of the long-standing debates among football fans has always been about the best runner—comparing the merits of the top runners of each era.

And so it goes. Was Jim Brown better than O. J. Simpson? Could Walter Payton have been a star in Red Grange's time? Would you rather have Earl Campbell in his prime or Eric Dickerson? Will Herschel Walker duplicate his USFL success in the NFL? How many yards would Gale Sayers have gained if he hadn't ripped up his knees?

Does this strike a familiar note? From the time Beattie Feathers became the NFL's first 1,000-yard rusher in 1934, the rushing record has been perhaps the sport's most popular standard and measuring stick.

When Feathers hit his 1,000, there were those who said it couldn't be done. And, indeed, it wasn't done again for 13 years. But the game was changing, and running backs were getting the ball more. Pretty soon the 1,000 yard runner had become commonplace, and fans began waiting for that first guy to crack 2,000.

O. J. Simpson showed the gridiron world that it could be done. Now, with a longer schedule and bigger, faster, stronger runners, where will the rushing record go? Will somebody hit 2,500 yards? Is 3,000 possible? Let's look at the anatomy of a record, how and when it was broken, and at the runners who came close, as well as those who went over the top.

In the early days of the game, runners just didn't get enough carries to rack up the kind of yardage they do today. That's in evidence by the yards-per-carry stats, which haven't changed much over the years. For example, Bill Osmanski of the Chicago Bears led the league in rushing in 1939 with 699 yards. But he only carried the ball 121 times, averaging 5.8 yards per carry. Powerful Marion Motley of Cleveland also averaged 5.8 yards per carry in 1950 when he led the league with 810 yards on 140 carries.

Ten years later the great Jim Brown averaged 5.8 yards a carry also. But his 1960 total was 1,257 yards, because he had 215 carries. By contrast, Walter Payton of the Bears averaged just 5.5 yards a carry in 1977, a little less than the others mentioned, but he gained 1,852 yards because he carried the ball 339 times. It must be remembered that the older backs also played defense. They were on the field for 60 minutes, so they couldn't be expected to carry the ball upwards of 300 times. Regardless, the guys who gain the big yards always capture the fancy of the fans.

When Beattie Feathers became the league's first 1,000-yard rusher in 1934, it wasn't that he got a lot of carries. Feathers lugged the ball only 101 times. It was just his year, and he broke one long run after another. His 1,004 yards came because of a record 9.94 yards per carry, a mark that still stands today.

Then the years passed without another back going over the 1,000-yard mark. Cliff Battles of Washington came close in 1937 when he got 874 yards on 216 carries. Some years, no one came close. The rushing leader in 1941 had just 486 yards, and two years later the top man got just 572 yards. But in 1945, a runner came along who looked as if he might threaten the record.

His name was Steve Van Buren, the Flying Dutchman, a man often called the first of the modern running backs. At six feet one inch and 200 pounds, Van Buren combined the speed of a sprinter, the agility of a dancer, and the straight-ahead power of a bruising fullback. He was a complete running back.

He joined the Philadelphia Eagles out of Louisiana State University in 1944. Though he played just four games and parts of two others that first year, Van Buren gained 444 yards, averaging five yards a carry. A year later he was up to 832 yards, averaging 5.8 a tote. Injuries limited him to just 529 yards in 1946, but a year

Steve Van Buren of the Philadelphia Eagles was considered the first of the great modern running backs. The Flying Dutchman combined speed and power when he set a rushing record of 1,146 yards on 263 carries in 1949.

later he began an assault on Beattie Feathers' rushing record.

It went down to the last game of the season, but Van Buren did it, running his total to 1,008 yards on 217 carries. Two years later he showed it wasn't a fluke, extending his record to 1,146 yards. This time he carried 263 times, averaging 4.4 yards a carry. That was a lot of leather lugging for a guy still playing full time on defense.

Injuries cut Van Buren's career short at the age of 31. Modern sports medicine undoubtedly could have added some years to it. But he retired as the NFL's career rushing leader in 1952. He also held the single season mark, and would for some time.

Van Buren's coach, Earl "Greasy" Neale, summed up his star running back's attributes: "He has the greatest head and shoulder fakes I've ever seen," Neale said. "He's better than (Red) Grange. Grange needed a blocker. The Dutchman doesn't. He can run away from tacklers, he can fake them, or he can run right over them."

In the ensuing years, more backs began approaching 1,000 yards, and several went over it. Joe "The Jet" Perry of San Francisco did it twice, and Rick Casares of the Bears did it once. But neither topped Van Buren's 1,146 yards. That was still the record.

Then along came Jim Brown. He joined the Cleveland Browns in 1957 after an All-American career at Syracuse University. Brown stood six foot two inches and weighed nearly 230 pounds. He was built like a block of granite, could run like the wind, or drag two or three tacklers along with him. Speed and power. That's the classic combination for a running back, and when it came to those qualities, Jim Brown wrote the book.

When he led the league in rushing his rookie year with 948 yards on 202 carries, it was obvious that Steve Van Buren's rushing record wasn't going to stand much longer. Unlike Van Buren, Brown didn't have to play defense, so he could conserve himself for offense, and he gave it his all every time he carried the football.

It took just another year for Jim Brown to not only break the record, but also to obliterate it. Jim rushed the ball 257 times in 1958, gaining 1,527 yards, an average of 5.9 yards a carry. There were times when he simply appeared unstoppable. He never seemed to get tired and he never appeared to be hurt.

Dr. Victor Ippolito, the Browns' team doctor, explained why he felt Brown was so suited to his profession. "Jim Brown has remarkable bone and muscle structure," the doctor said. "Some players are powerful from their waist up or waist down. Jim is powerful both ways. He doesn't have a man-made body and he's never out of condition. Call him at any time of the year and tell him he's got to play a football game and you'll find him razor sharp."

It was apparent that Jim Brown was going to be the standard against which all other runners would be matched. He continued going over 1,000 yards and was already being called the greatest running back of all time. When the 1963 season rolled around, Jim Brown was 27 years old and in his prime. The Browns had released longtime coach Paul Brown and replaced him with Blanton Collier. Now Jim Brown was ready for the greatest season of his life.

The Browns swept their first six games without a loss, and Jim Brown was spearheading the attack, averaging nearly 160 yards a game. No back had ever come close to that kind of yardage. At that rate, he would have gone well over 2,000 yards, an unthinkable total at that time.

Though the team fell off somewhat in the second half, as did Jim, he still completed the greatest year a running back ever had. He had broken his own rushing record with an incredible 1,863 yards, achieved on 291 carries for an average of 6.4 yards a pop. It was amazing—a record some said would stand for years and years, and a record which once again stamped Jim Brown as simply the greatest.

He was almost as good the next two years, gaining 1,446 and 1,544 yards. The end of 1965 marked his ninth year in the league, his eighth as rushing champion. He also had the most career yards with 12,312, over 4,000 more than his nearest rival. And with his great physical condition, the not yet 30-year-old Brown could be expected to have several more outstanding years.

But in the offseason he had an offer to make a movie, and production ran late. The Browns wanted him in camp. Then he had an offer for another film. It was

**The Greatest.** Cleveland's Jim Brown, bruised and battered, blasts a pair of Packer defenders during a 1964 game.

obvious then that a second career was in the offing. He had to make a decision, and it shocked everyone. He announced his retirement from football at the age of 29. So his record was safe from the one man who was a threat to break it—Jim Brown.

Jim did go on to a successful film career. And in the end, it wasn't his numbers they remembered so much. It was the beauty of his style, the way he could shift gears in the open field. It was the way he got up slowly after a hit, and walked back to the huddle as if he couldn't go anymore. But then he would get the ball again and . . . whoosh. He was gone. He was strong enough to take on any tackler or group of tacklers, and fast enough to outrun any defensive back. That was Jim Brown. Simply, the greatest.

Brown's retirement in 1965 was a shock. The logical question was who would be the next great ballcarrier. His successor at Cleveland, Leroy Kelly, was an outstanding back, a 1,000-yard runner in his own right. But he never approached Brown's greatness or his numbers. Gale Sayers in Chicago was a dynamic halfback who was a threat to score from anywhere on the field. He set some great marks, but never approached the rushing record. He didn't get the carries, and knee injuries cut his career short.

As the great Jim Brown was playing in final pro football games in December of 1965, a young runner was setting records at City College of San Francisco, a two-year junior college. He had the unlikely name of Orenthal James Simpson, but everyone knew him as

O.J. In 1967, Simpson transferred to the University of Southern California, and at USC he was so great for two years that his name was on everyone's lips. "How many yards did O.J. get?" was the question asked every week by football fans across the country.

He got plenty. As a junior at Southern Cal, the "Juice," as he was also called, rambled for 1,543 yards on 291 carries. A year later, he was even better, gaining 1,880 yards on an unbelievable 383 carries. Diehard football fans couldn't believe it. If this guy had gained those yards in the pros, he'd have broken Brown's record. The six-foot-two-inch, 215-pound Simpson wasn't as big as Brown, but he was extremely fast and knew how to run. And he had the endurance to carry 30 to 35 times a game.

"He'll run as often as we need him to run," said his college coach, John McKay. "And the more he runs, the better he gets."

That was surely the mark of a great one. People couldn't wait to see the Juice do his thing in the pros. As for O.J., he wanted to play pro ball, all right, but he was hoping to do it in the warm climate of his native California. The problem was that the team with the number one draft choice in 1969 was the Buffalo Bills. Not only was the city of Buffalo one of the coldest in the league in the winter, but the Bills were coming off a 1–12–1 season. Not exactly winning football.

Sure enough, Buffalo tabbed the Juice. And instead of being the Second Coming of Jim Brown, O. J. Simpson settled down to three seasons of mediocrity. Of course, he was running behind an offensive line known jokingly as the "vanishing five." That didn't help, either. Nor did the fact that he wasn't getting the carries, just 181 and 183 his first and third years, and 120 his second year, when he was slowed by a knee injury. His best rushing total was 742 yards in 1971.

It didn't matter. After three years, there were people who felt that O.J. was one of those great college players who didn't quite make it in the pros. In fact, with his original contract up, many thought the Juice would refuse to re-sign with Buffalo. But he showed his great character by signing a new multi-year deal. It was helped by the return of Lou Saban as the Bills' coach. Saban had coached the team in the early days of the franchise and had been a big success. Upon returning, he promised to build his team's attack around the running of O. J. Simpson. The Juice couldn't have been happier.

"I came out of USC as a running back, but I just haven't had the opportunities that some of the other pro backs have had," the Juice said. "They carry the ball 50 to 100 times more a season than I do."

But with Lou Saban back, things changed. In the opening game of the 1972 season, the Juice ran for 138 yards on 29 carries. That was more like it. There were more good days as the year wore on. O.J. looked more and more like his old self. When the year ended, O. J. Simpson was the NFL's top rusher with 1,251 yards on 292 carries. The club was just 4–9–1, but they showed improvement, especially with O.J. once again the hub of the attack. But as good as he was, no one was prepared for what was to happen in 1973.

Before the season started, O.J. told his friend, guard Reggie McKenzie, that he wanted to try for 1,700 yards.

"Why not make it 2,000?" McKenzie asked without hesitation.

"Why not?" O.J. answered.

The Bills opened the season at New England, and O.J. ran wild. He scored on touchdown runs of 80 and 22 yards, and when the game ended, he had set a record of 250 yards on 29 carries. With O.J. exploding, the Bills won easily, 31–13. New England coach Chuck Fairbanks couldn't say enough about the Juice.

"It looked like Grant going through Richmond," said Fairbanks. "We were helpless. No matter what we did we couldn't even slow him down, much less stop him."

That was just the beginning. In the ensuing weeks, O.J. ran for 103, 123, 171, and 166 yards. Then, after Miami held him to 55, he rebounded with 157 yards against Kansas City. At the halfway point of the season, he had 1,025 yards. Not only was he on the way to shattering Jim Brown's record, but he was on a 2,000 yard pace as well. Once again, O. J. Simpson had captured the fancy of the football world.

But the pace suddenly slowed. O.J. failed to gain 100 yards in the next two games, and while he rebounded for 120, 124, and 137 in the next three, he had given himself a tough nut to crack in the final two games.

After 12 games, he had 1,584 yards, leaving himself 280 yards short of breaking Brown's record. It wouldn't be easy. And he was also more than 400 yards shy of 2,000. That seemed next to impossible. In addition, the Bills were still in the hunt for a possible playoff berth. So that made game 13 against New England all the more important.

Playing on a snow-covered field that would have slowed many backs, O.J. just glided. He ripped off one big gain after another, as the New England defenders tried once more in vain to stop him. The results were almost as devastating for the Patriots as the opening game. O.J. gained 219 yards on just 22 carries and exploded into the national headlines once again.

He now had 1,803 yards, just 60 yards short of tying Jim Brown. He was also within 197 yards of 2,000, and the season finale in New York against the Jets would be the focus of national attention. The game was played at Shea Stadium on December 16, a cold, gray, snowy afternoon. But it promised to heat up once O.J. got the football.

With his offensive line all psyched, and the game plan geared for him to break the record, O.J. went to work. On the second play from scrimmage, O.J. swept around the right end for 30 yards. He wasn't wasting any time. He might have broken the record on that run if he hadn't slipped on the snowy turf at the 34. But quarterback Joe Ferguson kept calling the Juice's number and five plays later he ran for six yards, which left him just four yards shy of the rushing record.

70

This is the great O. J. Simpson on his way to a record-breaking 2,003 yards against the New York Jets in the snows of Shea Stadium in December of 1973.

Buffalo scored on the next play, so the Juice would have to wait until the next series.

It didn't take long. When the Bills got the ball back, O.J. got the call and promptly gained six yards. He had broken Jim Brown's record! But the game still wasn't over. Near the half, O.J. rambled 13 yards for a touchdown. A long punt return gave the Bills another score. They had a 21–7 halftime lead and O.J. Simpson had 1,910 yards. Could he top 2,000?

Once again, quarterback Ferguson began calling O.J.'s number. The going was slow and the snow was falling more heavily. A 25-yard gallop brought him within 50 yards of the magic mark. His teammates were all working with him now. He got eight yards, then 22, then nine, then five more. Suddenly, he was knocking at the door with 1,996 yards. With the snow continuing to fall, O.J. got the ball for the 34th time. He burst through the Jets' line behind a McKenzie block and gained another seven yards.

That did it. He had gained 2,003 yards for the season, and left the game, having carried for 200 more yards on this final day of the season. The Bills won the game to finish at 9–5. Though they just missed the playoffs, no one could blame O. J. Simpson. He had played his heart out, carrying the football for a record 332 times and averaging 6.0 yards a carry. Plus, he had broken the most glamorous record in the game.

O.J. continued to play brilliant football. Two years later, he gained 1,817 yards and the year after that 1,503. In 1976, he set another record by churning out 273 yards in a single game. Like Jim Brown, he finally left football for a career in front of the camera, and also like Brown, he left behind a brilliant record for others to chase. How long could it last this time?

Believe it or not, there was a run at the record within four years. The player threatening to break it was Walter Payton, a third-year halfback for the Chicago Bears. Payton came out of Jackson State University in 1975, as the Bears' top draft choice. He was expected to continue the tradition of great running in Chicago, where he'd be following in the footsteps of Red Grange, Bronko Nagurski, George McAfee, Rich Casares, Willie Galimore, and Gale Sayers.

At five feet ten inches, about 205 pounds, Walter Payton is a rock-solid player who always keeps himself in marvelous physical condition. In fact, when Chicago's backfield coach, Fred O'Connor, saw Walter for the first time, he made a now classic comment:

"I saw him stripped down in the lockerroom," said O'Connor, "and I thought, God must have taken a chisel and said, 'I'm gonna make me a halfback.'"

But the young halfback with the broad shoulders and muscular build had some troubles in his rookie year. In his very first game, he carried the ball eight times for a net of . . . nothing. Zero. He wasn't credited with a single yard. It was a debut he'd probably like to forget. Things got better after that, but when the season ended, the Bears were just a 4–10 team, and Walter had gained 679 yards on 196 carries for a 3.5 average.

It wasn't a bad first year, but many thought a number-one draft choice should have done better. True, Walter showed his versatility by catching 33 passes for another 213 yards, so those in the know realized the Bears had a great talent in their backfield. The very next year that talent began to emerge.

Walter started making noise the second week of the

season when he ran for 148 yards on 28 carries against the 49ers. Two weeks later, he gained 104 yards in a game with Washington, and a week after that he shredded a rugged Viking defense for 141 yards on just 19 carries. Walter Payton had obviously arrived.

He continued to play extremely well and in the tenth game of the season went over 1,000 yards for the first time. When he rambled for 183 yards against the Seahawks in the thirteenth game, he had 1,341 yards for the season, and he had broken Gale Sayers' team rushing record. That same afternoon, O. J. Simpson ran for 203 yards against Miami. With one week remaining, Walter led O.J. by nine yards in the race to become the NFL rushing champion.

It was a kind of last hurrah for the veteran Simpson, trying to hold off his heir apparent one more time. He did it, gaining 171 yards against Baltimore to finish with 1,503. Walter, in the meantime, had only 49 yards against the Broncos when he was injured in the third quarter and had to leave the game. Still, it was a great year. He finished with 1,390 yards on 311 carries and a 4.5 average.

Not winning the rushing title was a letdown, but Walter Payton was an All-Pro as well as *Sporting News* NFC Player of the Year in just his second season. And in 1977, he would really begin to strut his stuff with the best of them.

When Walter started the next year with 160 yards against Detroit, it was as if he was telling the world what to expect. In week number seven, he ran for 205

The NFL's all-time rushing leader, Walter Payton, showing his unique style of holding the football in one hand. Note the nickname "Sweetness" on the towel in front of his football pants.

yards on just 23 carries against Green Bay, and two weeks later had 192 yards versus Kansas City. After just nine games, Walter had gained 1,128 yards. How far could he go?

He tried to answer that the next week against Minnesota. Saddled with the flu, Walter was having hot and cold flashes before the game and feeling weak. But he decided to give it a try, and what he did that day will never be forgotten. Walter carried the ball 40 times and gained a record 275 yards, breaking the mark of 273 set just a year earlier by . . . you guessed it, O. J. Simpson. More important, the Bears won the game, 10–7, and afterward reporters asked Walter how he could do it with a bad case of the flu.

"If the game had gone into overtime, I imagine I could have gone some more," he said.

He now had 1,404 yards in 10 games. When O.J. gained his 2,003 yards in '73, he had just 1,323 in 10 games. So Walter was running ahead of O.J.'s pace. But, remember, the Juice closed with back-to-back 200-yard games. So it still wouldn't be easy, but Walter was giving it a try.

The next week he got 137, then 101. So with two games left, he needed 362 yards. When he ran for 163 against the Packers, he left himself a shot, though he still needed 200 yards in the finale against the New York Giants. His offensive line wanted to get it for him, just as O.J.'s had four years earlier. It was possible, all right, until the weather took a hand.

It began raining that morning, but no one was too concerned, because rain didn't usually affect the footing on the artificial turf at Giants Stadium. But soon the rain turned to hail and sleet. When the teams came out, the field was covered with ice, slush, and water—in other words, it was a mess. And it kept getting worse as the game wore on.

As it turned out, the weather made the game a sloppy one. The Bears won it, 6–3, and Walter managed just 47 yards on 15 tries. He fell short, gaining 1,852 yards on a record 339 carries and a 5.5 average. It was the third highest total in NFL history. Had it not been for the weather, Walter would undoubtedly have passed Jim Brown for second best.

But sing no sad songs for Walter Payton. He has been perhaps the NFL's most consistent and durable back ever, still going strong into his 30s. At the end of the 1986 season, he was the game's all-time leading rusher with 16,193 yards, almost 4,000 more than runner-up Brown. He's done that on a record 3,692 carries. And with all that running, he's never been seriously hurt, an amazing feat for a running back. No wonder he's a super record breaker.

Yet with all Walter Payton's achievements, O.J.'s single-season rushing record still stood. Three years after Payton tried to break it in 1980, there was yet another major challenge. This one came from a strong-legged fullback from Texas, Earl Campbell.

A five-foot-eleven-inch, 225-pound powerhouse, Campbell came out of Texas as the Heisman Trophy winner to join the Houston Oilers in 1978. Using the classic combination of speed and power, he promptly set a rookie rushing record with 1,450 yards on 302 carries. A year later, he was even better, running for 1,697 yards on 368 carries. Just how good could he be?

Campbell actually got off to a slow start in 1980. He had just 57 yards in the opener, 108 the next week, but only 11 yards when he was injured early in game three. Not the kind of stuff records are made of. He came back the next week but gained just 50 yards. After four games, he wasn't even among the top rushers.

Then it started happening. First there was a 178 yard day against Kansas City. Next a career high 203 yards against Tampa Bay. He followed that by running through Cincinnati to the tune of 202 yards. That made him just the second back in NFL history to put together back-to-back 200-yard games. The other was O.J. Simpson. (It's funny how that name keeps popping up.)

A week later, he had 157 yards for a total of 964 in nine games. He was coming on strong and talk began that Earl Campbell now had a shot at 2,000 yards and the record. After gaining 130 yards against New England, he produced his third 200-yard game of the season, rolling for 206 in 31 tries against the Bears. He did it with a dramatic 48-yard scamper in the final minute. He now had 1,300 yards after 11 games.

He was slowed by a bruised thigh against the Jets and got just 60 yards, then came back with 109 versus Cleveland. That seemed to pretty much finish him for the record, except for one thing. The schedule had been increased to 16 games in 1978, so he had two extra games to do it.

After 81 yards against Pittsburgh in the fourteenth game, Campbell made the most of the last two. He ran for 181 yards on 36 carries against Green Bay, then set a record of his own with his fourth 200-yard game of the season. He got 203 in the finale with Minnesota. But he didn't quite catch O.J.

Earl Campbell finished the year with 1,934 yards, the second best total in NFL history. He did it on 373 big carries and managed a fine 5.2 average. It seems the backs were carrying more and more. But O.J.'s record continued to endure.

Then, in 1983, came Eric Dickerson. He was a six-foot-three-inch 220-pounder out of Southern Methodist University—a big, strong, fast, and durable back who fit right into the L.A. Rams I-formation offense. The Rams knew they had a gun and they began firing. As a rookie, Dickerson set records with 390 carries and

**L.A. Rams tailback Eric Dickerson in action against the Houston Oilers during his record-breaking 1984 season. Dickerson ran for 2,105 yards, breaking the previous mark set by O. J. Simpson in 1973.**

1,808 yards gained. The yardage was a rookie record, the carries an all-time mark (since broken by James Wilder's 407 carries in 1984). There was little doubt Dickerson was the real thing. Now *he* was given the best chance of topping O.J.

Dickerson's first six games of '84 were solid, if not spectacular. His rushing totals read 138, 102, 49, 89, 120, and 107. He picked up the pace with 175 against New Orleans, and 145 yards versus Atlanta. After the 49ers held him to just 38 yards, Dickerson bounced back with a big 208-yard day on 21 carries against the Cardinals. He was leading the league in rushing, and with the 16-game slate, there were some who thought he had a chance to break the record.

His next four games produced some beautiful running. Dickerson is a glider. As the deep back in the I-formation, he can see the blocking patterns and the holes develop. Once he glides through, he has the ability to turn it on, to shift to another gear. He also has the running back's instinct to find the path of least resistance, whether it be to cut to the sideline or power straight into the secondary. All these skills produced games of 149, 132, 191, and 149 yards.

After 14 games, Eric Dickerson had 1,792 yards on 326 carries. Some people were quick to point out that O.J. had his 2,003 yards in 14 games. But a season's rushing record counts no matter how many games are in the season. And given the extra chance, Dickerson made the most of it. Playing against Houston, he was brilliant, racking up 215 yards on 27 carries. His final carry that day netted nine yards, and not only took him past 2,000, but brought him to 2,007 yards, four better than O.J. Eric Dickerson was the NFL's new single season rushing leader!

He gained 98 yards in the final game that year, finishing with a total of 2,105 yards on 379 tries, good for a 5.6 average. Comparisons are inevitable. Whether you think Dickerson is better than Simpson, or Simpson is better than Payton, or Payton is better than Brown doesn't really matter. All the great ones are great in their own right. Eric Dickerson isn't a fluke. He got a late start in '85 because of a salary squabble, but still gained 1,234 yards. Then in '86, he showed his great form once more, churning out 1,821 yards on an amazing 404 carries. He can lug the pigskin.

Just how far will the record go? It's come a long way since Beattie Feathers broke the 1,000-yard barrier back in 1934. Will Eric Dickerson take it even higher? Or perhaps the next record breaker will be young Herschel Walker of Dallas. Playing in the United States Football League in 1985, Walker gained 2,411 yards in 18 games. Unfortunately, the NFL does not recognize USFL records, and that league is now defunct.

One thing is certain—someone will do it. And the excitement of the chase will be there, as it has always been. For the man going after the rushing record is always in the spotlight and always on the spot. But no matter how great the pressure, he must continue to do what he does best . . . get that football and run it to daylight.

# A Perfect Season

A perfect season! Imagine that. Imagine a team going through an entire year without losing a game in the regular season or playoffs. Not only are you a champion, but you're a champion with an unblemished record. Now that's an accomplishment that merits bragging rights. A quick trip to the NFL record book will tell you which teams qualify.

Going way, way back to 1922, only the second season of the league that was to become the NFL, a team named the Canton (Ohio) Bulldogs didn't lose a game. They won ten, but alas, they tied a pair. They weren't perfect. Neither were the 1923 Bulldogs, a team that won 11 without a loss. They only tied one. Not perfect.

The Green Bay Packers of 1929 did the same thing—won 12, but tied one. Then there were the Chicago Bears. They finished with perfect records twice, in 1934 and again in 1942. But by then, there were two divisions and thus a title game. In both those years, the

Bears lost that championship contest. Still no perfect season.

There were a number of teams that lost just once. That's a great accomplishment in itself. Think about it. First of all, football is the only sport that holds the chance for a perfect season. It can't be done in baseball, with its 162-game schedule, or in basketball and hockey, where they play some 80-odd games. But in football, with 12, then 14, and now 16-game schedules, then two or three playoff games . . . well, it's possible. And, yes, it has been done.

Welcome to the 1972 Miami Dolphins, a franchise that had just been born in 1966. They were an expansion team with an expansion record those first few years. But by 1970, the Dolphins surprised everyone by finishing 10–4 and making the playoffs for the first time. A year later, they took the AFC Eastern title for the first time and went all the way to the Super Bowl before they lost to Dallas, 24–3.

So in 1972, the Dolphins were one of the favorites to be in the super hunt again. They had a topnotch quarterback in Bob Griese and a good backup in veteran Earl Morrall. The runners were outstanding with bruising fullback Larry Csonka, halfbacks Jim Kiick and Mercury Morris. Paul Warfield was an All-Pro wide receiver, while Marv Fleming was a tough, experienced tight end.

The offensive line was rock solid, with guards Larry Little and Bob Kuechenberg considered the best in the league. The team had a no-name defense, but there were some real solid players, like middle linebacker Nick Buoniconti, and safeties Jake Scott and Dick Anderson. This was a very good football team, and their coach, Don Shula, was considered one of the best in the business. The Dolphins were good, but no one really knew how good.

Game number one at Kansas City set the tone. The Dolphins won it, 20–10, with Griese completing eight of 15 passes for one score, while Csonka churned out 118 yards and Morris 67. The defense did the rest. That was Dolphin football. Quarterback Griese rarely put the ball up 35–45 times like so many quarterbacks of today. The team preferred a conservative, ball-control approach. But they had the talent to open it up when necessary.

After an easy 34–13 victory over Houston, the Dolphins proved their mettle for the first time. Trailing the Vikings, 14–6, midway through the final quarter, they drew closer when Garo Yepremian booted a 51-yard field goal. Then, in the closing minutes, Bob Griese led the team on a drive through the tough Minnesota defense. With the ball on the three and just seconds remaining, Griese rolled to his right and flipped a pass to tight end Jim Mandich in the end zone. They had pulled it out, 16–14, to run their record to 3–0.

Next came a victory over the Jets, then a game against San Diego back in Miami at the Orange Bowl. Early in the game, quarterback Griese rolled out to his left, looking for a receiver. As he released the ball, he was hit by two huge Charger linemen. He went down and didn't get up. Onto the field came thirty-nine-year-old Earl Morrall. He would have to take over as Griese was carried off on a stretcher. Would the Dolphins' season go down the tubes?

The verdict for Griese wasn't good. He had a double injury: a dislocated ankle and a broken bone several inches above the ankle. But he was glad to hear that Morrall had completed eight of 10 passes in a 24–10 Dolphin victory. The team was still unbeaten at 5–0, but how far could they go with a 39-year-old quarterback who now had to carry the whole load?

There was a scare the following week, but the Dolphins and Morrall squeezed past Buffalo, 24–23. After that, the veteran Morrall seemed to settle in and the club rolled. They shut out Baltimore, whipped Buffalo again, then steamrolled New England, 52–0. After they toppled the Jets by four points, they had an easy win over St. Louis, 31–10.

By now, the Dolphins were becoming the talk of the football world. They had a perfect 11–0 record with three games left. What's more, they had won seven in a row since their starting quarterback went down. But the running attack had been outstanding with the pile-driving strength of Csonka, the steadiness of Kiick, and the explosive outside speed of Morris. Morrall had proven to be an experienced leader who kept mistakes to a minimum.

Then the Dolphins whipped New England, 37–21, and the Giants, 23–13. They stood at 13–0 and needed one more win to become the first NFL team to post a perfect regular season record since the 1942 Bears 30 years earlier. And there was more good news. Bob Griese would be available for spot duty in the season finale against Baltimore. If nothing else, he was expected to give the team a psychological lift.

The Dolphins wasted little time in striking. Yepremian started things off with a 40-yard field goal in the opening session. In the second quarter, Morrall tossed a 14-yard TD pass to Warfield. Two more Yepremian field goals highlighted the third period. With the no-name defense putting a blanket on the Baltimore offense, the Dolphins held a 16–0 lead going into the final session.

That gave Coach Shula a chance to get Bob Griese back into action. Griese played it safe in his return, calling a ball-control game and letting his defense do the rest. The Dolphins won it, 16–0. They were undefeated for the season. But completing the unbeaten season wouldn't be easy. Unlike the old days, when there was a single championship game, the Dolphins would have to endure a divisional playoff, then the AFC championship, and finally the Super Bowl. That is, of course, if they continued winning.

In the first playoff game against the Cleveland Browns, the Dolphins found their character tested once again. With the veteran Morrall still at quarterback, they took an early lead, scoring on a blocked punt and a Yepremian field goal. That made it 10–0, a

The essence of the unbeaten Miami Dolphins of 1972 can be seen right here. Quarterback Earl Morrall hands to his halfback Jim Kiick, who runs for daylight behind bruising fullback Larry Csonka. The Dolphins parlayed this ball-control offense into the only perfect season in NFL history.

score that held until the half. Most fans figured the no-name defense would take care of the rest.

But in the third quarter, the Browns fought back. First they made it 10–7. Another Yepremian field goal upped it to 13–7 early in the fourth quarter. But a Mike Phipps to Fair Hooker pass midway through the period resulted in a 27-yard touchdown. Suddenly, for one of the few times all year, the Dolphins found themselves behind late in the game, 14–13.

With the fans in the Orange Bowl screaming for Bob Griese, Coach Shula stuck with the veteran Morrall. There were less than five minutes remaining when the Dolphins began to move. A pair of Morrall to Paul Warfield passes covered some 50 yards. A penalty brought the ball to the Cleveland eight, and from there, Jim Kiick powered over the goal line. Yepremian's kick made it a 20–14 game.

The Browns tried one last drive, but a clutch interception by linebacker Doug Swift ended the threat. From there, the Dolphins ran out the clock. They had their fifteenth straight win and were now in the AFC title game against the improving Pittsburgh Steelers.

This one was played at Three Rivers Stadium in Pittsburgh, so the Dolphins would be facing a hostile crowd as well as a tough team. They were thinking Super Bowl now, world's championship, but they also had to have that undefeated season on their minds. And they knew it still wouldn't be easy.

Pittsburgh intercepted a Morrall pass early in the opening period and promptly marched downfield for a score. So once again the Dolphins found themselves playing from behind. A fake punt by Larry Seiple gave the Dolphins life in the second period. Seiple ran the ball from his own 38 all the way to the Pittsburgh 12. From there, Morrall took the team in, throwing nine yards to Csonka for the score. The kick tied the game at 7–7, and that's how the half ended.

Before the second half began, Coach Shula made a big decision, even a gamble. He decided to insert Bob Griese at quarterback, in the hope of giving the offense a lift. But it was the Steelers who scored first on a Roy Gerela field goal to take a 10–7 lead. Now Griese had to bring the team back.

He did it by going to his favorite receiver, Paul Warfield, on a 52-yard bomb that brought the ball to the Steeler 24. Six plays later, Jim Kiick scored and the extra point made it a 14–10 game. A fourth-quarter drive resulted in another score, and while a final Steeler touchdown made it close, the Dolphins had taken the AFC title, 21–17. And they were still undefeated, with only the Super Bowl remaining.

In the super game, the Dolphins would be facing the Washington Redskins, a tough team that had compiled an 11–3 mark during the regular season, then had beaten Green Bay and Dallas to reach the big one. But the Dolphins were ready. Bob Griese was at the helm again and they went to work.

A Griese to Howard Twilley pass gave the Dolphins a 7–0 lead at the end of the first quarter. In the second period, Griese engineered another drive. He kept the ball on the ground, letting fullback Csonka do the bulk of the work. Then, from the Redskin 21, he fired a pass to Jim Mandich, who made a diving catch at the two. Jim Kiick ran it in for the score and Yepremian's kick made it a 14–0 game.

From there, the defenses took over, and it stayed that way until the fourth period when the Skins scored on a fumble recovery and run by defensive back Mike Bass. That made it 14–7, but the Dolphin defense would give up no more. Miami won the game, and the Super Bowl, and got themselves into the record books at the same time.

The club had won all of its 17 games. No ties, no losses. A notable achievement. All it would have taken was one off day for Griese or Morrall, one defensive breakdown at the wrong time, or just one bad bounce of the football, and no unbeaten year. But the Miami Dolphins of 1972 did it, setting a record that can never be broken—only tied.

# How About a Few "Mosts"?

There is a pecking order to any record book. Take a record and you start with the guy at the top. Maybe the next guy was the one whose record was broken. Or, then again, he may be the guy who almost broke the record. If a record is broken, the pecking order changes. There is a new man at the top, a new man who has the most. He is the target of the next group of potential record breakers.

Let's look at some "mosts" from the NFL record book. Some of them are simply amazing because it's hard to believe a player could be that good. But remember again, they say that records are made to be broken.

When Fran Tarkenton joined the Minnesota Vikings in 1961, they said he'd never make it. For one thing, he was small for a quarterback. Tarkenton stood a shade over six feet and weighed in the neighborhood of 180 pounds. Quarterbacks were supposed to be bigger than that.

Plus, he was a scrambler. That was unheard of in the National Football League of the early 1960s. Quarterbacks were supposed to drop straight back, protected in a "pocket" of offensive linemen and backs, look downfield for a receiver, and throw. Fran Tarkenton didn't do this. Playing for the expansionist Vikings, there was never much of a pocket, and Fran Tarkenton often had to run for his life.

Soon, scrambling became his style, and it drove defensive linemen crazy. They would wear themselves out chasing Fran Tarkenton all over the field. Listen to Hall of Fame defensive end Gino Marchetti, who played with the Baltimore Colts. Marchetti was used to chasing the standard drop-back passer.

"We were going up against this young kid and I thought it would be easy," said Gino. "Then he started running around back there. I had him one time, I thought. . . . So I really cut loose and what happens? He's going the other way and I'm tackling air. It was like he had eyes in the back of his head . . . unless he heard me huffing and puffing behind him."

Then they said he'd get hurt, running around like that. Well, Fran played from 1961 to 1978 and was only hurt once, and that came very late in his career. He was as durable a quarterback as there ever was. Then they said he didn't have the arm, that he was just a short to medium thrower. Maybe he didn't have a cannon hanging off his shoulder, but he knew how to get the job

Minnesota's Fran Tarkenton dropping back to pass was a sight that often drove opponents to distraction. The first "scrambling" quarterback would often run all over the field before getting a pass off, as the opposition huffed and puffed trying to catch him.

done. Oh, did he know how. When he finally retired after the 1978 season, he left behind a legacy that still stands today.

Fran Tarkenton threw more passes (6,467) than any other quarterback in history. He also completed more (3,686) and amassed the most yardage in NFL annals, some 47,003 yards passing. He also has the most lifetime touchdown passes, having connected for scores on 342 occasions. So while Fran Tarkenton might not have been the greatest quarterback who ever lived, he was certainly doing something right.

After all, when he came up, the purists said a team could never win with a scrambler as quarterback. Once again, Fran Tarkenton proved them wrong. He made the expansionist Vikings respectable, then went to the New York Giants where he made a poor team competitive. And when he returned to the Vikings, he helped lead them into the Super Bowl three different times.

That was Fran Tarkenton, the scrambler, and a record breaker for sure.

He had a great name for a wide receiver. Tom Fears. And he did indeed strike fear in the hearts of defensive backs who tried to cover him during his career with the Los Angeles Rams, which lasted from 1948 to 1956. He was part of some great championship Rams teams, and teamed with Elroy (Crazylegs) Hirsch to form an explosive receiving tandem.

The Rams had a great team then, balanced on offense and defense. They even had two number one quarterbacks for a number of those years. Both Bob Waterfield and Norm Van Brocklin could air it out and win it for you, especially if they were throwing to Fears and Hirsch. Just to prove what a devastating quartet they made, all four players (Fears, Hirsch, Waterfield, and Van Brocklin) are in pro football's Hall of Fame.

But the day that really belonged to Tom Fears was December 3, 1950, as the Rams hosted the Green Bay Packers at the Los Angeles Coliseum. It was a defensive battle early on, and it took the Rams a while to get the offense in gear. They didn't score in the first period, but in the second, former Army All-American Glenn Davis scored a pair of touchdowns on a four-yard run and nine-yard pass reception from Van Brocklin. At the half, it was just a 16–7 game.

Then in the third period, the Rams opened up. Alternating quarterbacks, they took to the air, with Fears getting open time and again. Van Brocklin connected with Fears for an 11-yard score in the third period, then hit Hirsch from 37 yards out.

In the fourth period, the Rams controlled the football, and surprisingly, they did it by passing, much like some of today's teams prefer. Both QB's looked for Fears as their primary receiver. Always a great deep threat, Fears was catching a brace of short and medium range passes this day. Waterfield hit him for another score from four yards out, and when the game ended, the Rams had a 51–14 victory.

Van Brocklin had thrown for 212 yards and three scores, while Waterfield had 139 air yards and a pair of TD's. But the big news was Tom Fears. He had set a new National Football League record by catching 18 passes for a total of 189 yards. Ten of his receptions came in the final period as the Packer defenders just could not stop him.

Tom Fears is long retired, a Hall of Famer, yet his

record lives on. He's still got the most receptions in a game. Only the pecking order below him has changed. In September 1980, New York Jets' halfback Clark Gaines challenged Fears' mark, but came up one short. And back in November of 1962, St. Louis wide receiver Sonny Randle had a big day and wound up with 16 catches. They came close, but Tom Fears still reigns supreme.

They called him the Golden Boy because of his blond hair and his reputation as a man about town. But Paul Hornung was all football player. It just took some foresight by his coach, the legendary Vince Lombardi, to harness his talents in the right direction.

Hornung came out of Notre Dame in 1957, a quarterback and Heisman Trophy winner, and that supposedly made him the best college player in the land. But when he joined the Green Bay Packers, he found that things were different. He had been the glamour player on perhaps the most glamorous college team of them all. Suddenly, he was a struggling rookie quarterback with one of the worst teams in the NFL.

As the Packers staggered through 3–9 and 1–10–1 seasons in '57 and '58, Paul Hornung slowly came to a very frightening realization. Despite playing the position all his life, he didn't have what it takes to be a pro quarterback. And when the team hired a new coach prior to the 1959 season, Hornung wasn't sure what fate awaited him.

That coach was Vince Lombardi, and the first day he

met with his new team, Lombardi supposedly picked up a football and said, "Gentlemen, this is a football. Before we're through we're gonna run it down everybody's throat."

A stern taskmaster, determined to keep his word, Lombardi went to work. His first task was to evaluate Packer personnel and get rid of the deadwood and stragglers. And pretty soon he had to answer an obvious question: What to do with Paul Hornung? He had already settled on Bart Starr as his quarterback. But it didn't take Coach Lombardi long to find the answer. He approached Hornung.

"The way I use an offense," he said, "I need a hard-running halfback who can pass every now and then. You're it. Just as long as you can hold it."

For the six-foot-two-inch, 215-pound Hornung, this was the perfect solution. Teamed with bruising fullback Jim Taylor, Hornung helped give the Packers a backfield tandem that would play a large role in the team's rapid transition to champions. And while Hornung never had the big stats, he was a winning ballplayer you could count on in the clutch. He knew how to score. Even Lombardi sensed it.

"In the middle of the field, he [Hornung] may be only slightly better than an average ballplayer," Lombardi said. "But inside that 20-yard line, he is one of the greatest I have ever seen. He smells that goal line."

Besides his running, receiving, and occasional passing, Paul Hornung did something else for the Packers, and that's what gave him his place in the record book.

He was their field goal and extra point kicker. As the Packers began approaching respectability in 1959, Hornung led the NFL in scoring with seven touchdowns, seven field goals, and 31 extra points good for 94 total points. That wasn't so great. The record at that time was 138 points, scored in 1942 by the great receiver, Don Hutson, also a Green Bay Packer.

But in 1960, Paul Hornung was to obliterate that mark. As the Packers clawed their way to their first Western Division title under Lombardi, finishing with an 8–4 mark, Paul Hornung set a mark that still stands.

In just 12 games, he scored 15 touchdowns and kicked 15 field goals and 41 conversions for a total of 176 points, the most ever scored in a single season. Prorated over today's 16-game slates, Hornung would have scored some 233 points. Yet in the years since, with 14 and 16 games slates, no one has topped the mark.

The closest to Hornung are Washington kicker Mark Moseley, who booted his way to 161 points in 1983; and Gino Cappelletti, a wide receiver and kicker for the old Boston Patriots. Cappelletti scored 155 points in 1964.

And for those who want to know if Hornung was the all-time scorer, the answer is no way. Only one man can possibly hold that distinction. He was George Blanda, who played a record 26 years of professional football. A quarterback and place kicker, Blanda has the most points ever scored, having tallied 2,002 points in his long career. That's another one that will be around for quite a while.

* * *

Who knows if Jim Bakken could make an NFL team if he were to try out today? After all, Bakken was an old-fashioned, straight-ahead placekicker, and like the Edsel, you don't see very many of them anymore. They have been replaced by the sidewinders, the soccer-style kickers who approach the ball at an angle and sweep their legs across their bodies. That's supposed to generate more power.

It seems odd, then, that so many of the kicking records are still held by the old straight-ahead booters. Maybe they didn't always get the distance, but many of them were very accurate.

And Jim Bakken was one of the best of his time. He was drafted by the Rams, but was soon released. The Cardinals then picked him up and he spent the bulk of his career with them. Bakken was a fine athlete who also practiced as a wide receiver in case of emergencies. But he was too valuable as a kicker to take a chance on injury elsewhere.

It was early in the '67 season when the Cardinals traveled to Pitt Stadium to meet the Steelers. Bakken, like the other kickers in the NFL, was well aware that a little, left-footed soccer-style kicker named Garo Yepremian had set a new record just a year earlier when he booted six field goals in a single game. Bakken had often thought about breaking the record, but he didn't think this September 24 afternoon would be the day.

"In practice, I didn't feel my leg was as strong as usual," Bakken said, "and the wind was really playing tricks with the ball. I thought for sure I was gonna have one of those days where nothing goes right."

Early in the first quarter, the Cards drove downfield and were stalled at the 11. Bakken came on to try an 18-yard field goal. The kick was perfect and the Cards had the lead. Minutes later, the Steelers fumbled the kickoff and the Cards got the ball back. Six plays later, Bakken kicked a 24-yarder and the Cards had a 6–0 lead.

"When you get two that fast, you begin to feel like Superman," Bakken said.

With his confidence high, Bakken watched his team score a touchdown and then booted the extra point. Then, early in the second period, he was just short on a 50-yard field goal try. But he didn't miss by much. Yet less than three minutes later, a Pat Fischer interception set the Cards up and Bakken booted a 33-yard three-pointer, his third of the game. The Cards now led 16–0.

The Steelers scored midway through the period to cut the lead to 16–7, but Bakken came on again before the half and was perfect on a 29-yarder. Field goal number four, and a 19–7 lead. In the third quarter, Pittsburgh scored again making it 19–14, and Bakken missed a 45-yarder by a matter of inches. He couldn't worry about records now, because the game was still up for grabs.

But with just 41 seconds gone in the fourth period, Bakken came on to boot a 24-yarder, his fifth field goal of the day. That gave the Cards a 22–14 lead, and when the Steelers tried to catch up, they were intercepted once more. The Cards drove down to the 26-yard line, then stalled. With 5:33 left in the game, Jim Bakken got ready to swing his right leg into the ball once again.

This one came from the 32. It was up . . . and good! Jim Bakken's sixth field goal had tied Yepremian's NFL record. The question now was whether he'd get a chance to break it. Once again, Bakken and the Cards got the big play. The Steelers were forced to punt and Roy Shivers brought the return all the way to the Pittsburgh 23-yard line.

Bakken could feel the butterflies as the Card offense moved the ball closer. They got to the 17 when Bakken was called upon again. The 23-yard field goal wasn't a long one, but Jim Bakken knew he was going for the record. He tried to force himself to concentrate as he stepped into the ball.

He was so anxious that he said he jerked his head up too soon to look at the ball. Fortunately, he had hit it well and the ball sailed through the uprights. Seven field goals in a game. A new NFL record, the most three-pointers ever kicked in a single game.

In the years since, a number of kickers have booted six in a game, including Jim Bakken, who did it in 1973. But no one has hit that seventh. Bakken stands alone, a record breaker with a mark to remember.

# Touchdown . . . Lenny Moore

That was a familiar cry of sports announcers for some 12 years between 1956 and 1968. Those were the years that Lenny Moore played for the Baltimore Colts. Moore was a complete halfback, a daring broken-field runner as well as a dangerous pass receiver. He was one of quarterback John Unitas' favorite targets, especially in game-breaking situations.

And Lenny Moore was tough. Despite weighing in the neighborhood of 190 pounds, the former Penn State All-American wasn't afraid to stick his head in there and take on the biggest defensive players. He was one of those guys who would have been a star in any era, but the fans of Baltimore didn't mind having him in the '50s and '60s. He played an integral role in the championship Baltimore clubs of 1958 and 1959, and the Western Conference titlists of 1964.

For all his diverse talents, it's not surprising that Lenny Moore set an incredible record, one that still stands today. What made it even more impressive was that Lenny set his mark at a time in his career when it appeared he was on the downslide, that injuries and bad luck were taking their toll.

It started after the 1961 season. Moore was brilliant that year, turning short passes into long gainers all year with his electrifying running. He came close to the single season records for touchdowns and all-around total yardage. He was an all-pro with a nearly seven-yard rushing average who finished in the top ten in both rushing and receiving, the only player to accomplish that in '61.

Then, in the final pre-season game of 1962, Moore cracked a kneecap. He was out six weeks and never regained his old form when he did get back. He was hoping to come all the way back in '63. But once again the final week before the season proved a jinx. This time he had an emergency appendectomy.

He came back a few weeks later, but had some problems adjusting to new coach Don Shula's system. Shula was using him more as a straight running back and less as a receiver. Then, in an October 27 game against Green Bay, Moore caught a 13-yard scoring pass from Unitas. A week later, against Chicago, he scored on a nifty 25-yard run. Then the week after, he ran for a four-yard touchdown against Detroit. But late in that game he sustained a severe kick in the head. He began suffering dizzy spells and the doctors recommended he sit out the final five weeks of the season.

So at the outset of the 1964 season, Lenny Moore felt he had a lot to prove. He showed he was ready in the opening game when he scored on a two-yard run,

**Hall-of-Fame halfback Lenny Moore poses for the camera prior to a pre-season workout in 1964. Equally dangerous as a runner or a receiver, Moore set a record by scoring touchdowns in 18 consecutive games.**

then broke one open with Unitas, scoring on a big 70-yard, pass-run play. A week later, he caught a 52-yard TD toss from Johnny U. and later bulled his way in from the four.

Against Chicago the following Sunday, he tallied from the three, then against the Rams he scored on runs of 12 and 32 yards. Lenny Moore was back, all right, playing brilliant football, and what's more, the Colts were once again looking like the best team in the league. It was also about that time when someone realized that Lenny Moore had a streak going. He had scored a touchdown in the final three games of 1963 in which he played. Now he had tallied in the first seven of '64. That made 10 straight games in which he had crossed the goal line.

The scoring streak continued. Lenny was delivering from in close and from far out. On November 15, he got his touchdown against Minnesota when he gathered in a 74-yard toss from Unitas. A week later against the Rams, it was on an 18-yard run. He already had the record for scoring in the most consecutive games, and now it stood at 14. He made it 15 at San Francisco the next week. Then came a December 6 game against Detroit.

This game might have signaled the end of the streak had it not been for Lenny Moore's great football instincts and quick reflexes. The Colts had the ball and quarterback Unitas went to wide receiver Jimmy Orr. Orr grabbed the pass at the Detroit 35 and began running toward the goal line. He had a good shot at a score.

But as he reached the five-yard line, he fumbled the ball. Another wide receiver, Raymond Berry, tried to grab the loose pigskin, but all he succeeded in doing was to knock the ball over the goal line into the end zone. A number of players on both sides lunged after the ball, but Baltimore's number 24 got there first. Lenny Moore was clutching the ball for a touchdown! It was the only one he was to score that day, and it ran his streak to 16 games.

A week later, he scored twice on a pair of short runs against Washington as the Colts finished the regular season with a 12–2 record and the conference title. Lenny Moore had turned in a great season, with 584 yards rushing and 472 receiving. His receiving yardage came on just 21 catches, an average of more than 22 yards a catch. He also set a new season record (since broken) with 20 touchdowns, and his TD streak was alive at 17 games.

The Colts lost in the championship game that year to the Cleveland Browns, 27–0. But that couldn't dim Lenny Moore's achievements. When he scored a touchdown on a one-yard run against Minnesota in the opening game of 1965, he ran his touchdown string to 18. It ended a week later when the Colts met the Packers and Moore was shut out.

Lenny Moore played through the 1967 season, and his career achievements were rewarded by his eventual election to pro football's Hall of Fame. A number of his records have since been broken, but the one that still stands is his 18-game touchdown streak.

It will definitely be a tough record to beat. In the years that have passed since Moore's streak, a couple of pretty fair football players have made a run at the mark and fallen short. The second longest streak now belongs to O. J. Simpson, who scored in 14 consecutive games with Buffalo in 1975. And the third best belongs to Washington fullback John Riggins, who scored in 13 straight in 1982 and 1983. They gave it a good try, but neither could catch Lenny Moore.

# Those Super Legs

There is no greater single event showcase in sports than the Super Bowl. The game is hyped for two weeks all around the land, then watched by millions upon millions of people. When a player excels in the Super Bowl, everyone knows it, because that player is on center stage for all to see.

Traditionally, the quarterback has been the glamour guy of the Super Bowl. In fact, in the 21 Super Bowls played through 1987, the QB has been the Most Valuable Player 11 times. And, indeed, there have been some brilliant quarterback performances in the big game. The remainder of the MVP prizes have been pretty much equally divided. There have been two wide receivers, one linebacker, one defensive back, three linemen, and four running backs.

Ah, yes, running backs. The guys who take the big pounding and don't always get the recognition. There have been some really big games by Super Bowl running backs, and the interesting part is that whenever a runner has produced a record-breaking game in the Super Bowl, his team has won the game.

Since Matt Snell of the New York Jets produced the first outstanding performance by a runner in Super Bowl III, the Super rushing record, set by Snell, has been broken five times. Let's take a look at each of these great running shows and see how they affected the outcome of the games.

The first two Super Bowls failed to produce a 100-yard rusher. The outcomes were decided by the passing arm of Green Bay Packer quarterback Bart Starr. Then, in Super Bowl III, the Baltimore Colts were overwhelming favorites to beat the upstart New York Jets. But the Jets' flamboyant young quarterback, Joe Namath, not only predicted a Jets win, he guaranteed it.

Early in the game, Namath felt his offensive line could dominate the defensive line of the Colts. He began using his outstanding fullback, Matt Snell, to prove his point. Snell was a big, strong, hard-hitting runner and he began making his presence felt. Late in the period, with the game still scoreless, the Jets got the ball at their own 20 following an interception.

Four straight times Namath had Snell run at the right side of the Colt defense and the big guy had the ball out to the Baltimore 46. A series of short passes brought the ball to the 21. Namath then hit Snell for a 12-yard gain. From the nine, the fullback smashed first to the five, then into the end zone, running over the Baltimore middle linebacker in the process. The conversion gave

**Fullback Matt Snell of the New York Giants was the first running back to crack 100 yards in a Super Bowl game. Snell gained 120 yards on 30 tries as the Jets shocked the football world with a 16–7 upset of the Baltimore Colts in Super Bowl III.**

the Jets a 7–0 lead and Matt Snell had set the tone of the game.

The Jets got a pair of field goals in the third period and one more in the fourth, taking a 16–0 lead before the Colts scored a lone touchdown late in the game to make it a 16–7 final. And Namath, wise beyond his years, ate up chunks of time by calling Snell's number again and again.

When it ended, the big guy had carried the football 30 times and gained 121 yards, a Super Bowl record. Namath was the MVP, but Matt Snell's running did as much as anything to help pull off perhaps pro football's biggest upset.

Matt Snell's Super Bowl rushing record lasted five years, until Super Bowl VIII, which matched the Miami Dolphins and Minnesota Vikings at Rice Stadium in Houston. The Dolphins were defending champs, having beaten Washington the year before, 14–7. They played a ball control game which often featured the running of fullback Larry Csonka.

Csonka had gained 112 yards the year before, missing Snell's record by just 10 yards. Chances were he'd get a lot of work again, especially if the Dolphins got the early lead. The big guy was a 245-pound piledriver capable of controlling a game. The Dolphins' coach, Don Shula, as well as quarterback Bob Griese were well aware of that.

The first time Miami got the ball they drove 62 yards in 10 plays. Griese mixed runs by Csonka and Mercury

Morris with short passes to Jim Mandich and Marlin Briscoe. The last play of the drive came from the five. Csonka took the ball, lowered his head, and plowed into the end zone. The kick made it 7–0.

Minutes later, they were at it again, this time a 66-yard march with the same mix of plays. Jim Kiick scored from the one and it was a 14–0 game after Yepremian's kick. In the second period, a Miami field

Bruising fullback Larry Csonka was a mainstay of the Miami Dolphin offense in the mid-1970s. Csonka had one of his greatest days against the Minnesota Vikings in Super Bowl VIII. Miami won the game 24–7, and Csonka set a then–Super Bowl rushing record of 145 yards on 33 carries.

goal made it 17–0. When the Dolphins scored early in the third period to lead 24–0, it was all but over. The Dolphins were too good a team to let a lead like that slip away.

Fullback Csonka had been a workhorse all afternoon, and the further Miami got ahead, the more he carried the ball to eat up the clock. A Minnesota score late in the game didn't matter. Miami won it, 24–7.

Along the way, Larry Csonka rewrote the Super Bowl running book. He had carried the ball 33 times for a record 145 yards, and was named the game's Most Valuable Player.

"Csonka has run that hard before," said Minnesota Coach Bud Grant, not surprised that the big fullback had done so well. "When Miami gets ahead of you, Csonka is going to carry the ball 25 times. This is one of their strengths."

So once again, it was a matter of a fullback controlling a game. Larry Csonka's big day certainly paid off for the Dolphins.

But Larry Csonka didn't really get to enjoy his Super Bowl record for long. The very next year another fullback came along to have an even better day in the Super Bowl. It was Super Bowl IX and the Minnesota Vikings were back hoping to avenge their loss to Miami the year before. This time their opponents were the Pittsburgh Steelers, a team on the rise and a team hungry to win its first championship in 42 years.

The strength of the Steelers was their defense, but the offense had the potential to explode. Their two most well-known performers at this point were quarterback Terry Bradshaw and fullback Franco Harris. Bradshaw had been in a fight for the starter's job early in the season and was still readjusting to his role. Harris had a fine year, but in the week prior to the Super Bowl he had been suffering from a bad head cold.

In the first quarter, the game was a defensive struggle. Neither team could get a sustained drive going. The Steelers were running the ball and Franco Harris didn't seem to be showing the effects of his cold. He was gaining good yardage, but the Viking defense was tough. The game was scoreless after one, and the only score in the second period was a Pittsburgh safety. So the Steelers took a 2–0 lead into the lockerroom.

In the second half, Franco began making his presence felt. The Steelers got the ball on a recovered fumble at the Vikings' 30. The big fullback then ran around the left end for 24 yards to the six. After losing three, he swept the left end again and this time went nine yards into the end zone for the score. The kick made it a 9–0 game. That's how the third quarter ended.

The Vikings finally scored on the recovery of a blocked punt in the end zone. The extra point was missed, but the game was now a close one at 9–6. With more than 10 minutes still remaining, the Steelers had the ball at their own 34 and began driving. So Franco Harris was doing more than run out the clock.

As the Steelers began driving, quarterback Bradshaw continued to go to the big guy, who was ripping off the yardage. Like all of the great ones, Franco got stronger as the game went on, and unlike other fullbacks, he had the speed to get outside and outrun smaller defensive backs.

His running helped the Steelers bring it to the four. Then Bradshaw hit tight end Larry Borwn for the score. The kick made it a 16–6 game. Then the Steelers ran out the clock, again using Franco Harris. He had carried the ball six times during the final touchdown drive, and he got it five more times before the game ended.

On his 34th and final carry of the afternoon, Franco Harris had enough left to skirt the right end for 15 big yards. That enabled him to burst past Larry Csonka and set a new Super Bowl rushing mark. Franco had carried 34 times for 158 yards and was named the game's MVP.

When told he had run for 158 yards, Franco said, "You've got to be kidding!" Then he added, "Gaining 1,000 yards [during the regular season] and contributing to a title and Super Bowl victory make this the most significant year of my career."

Franco Harris was to become football's third all-time leading rusher before retiring. But of all the great days he had on the gridiron, his Super Bowl rushing record had to be one of the most memorable.

* * *

It would be eight years before another running back would challenge the Super Bowl rushing record of Franco Harris. In that time, a couple of wide receivers had been the MVP's, then a couple of linemen, and finally four straight quarterbacks. The QB's seemed to be dominating the Super Bowl once again.

But in Super Bowl XVII, things changed. It came after the strike-shortened season of 1982. There was a special Super Bowl tournament that year and the survivors were the Washington Redskins of the NFC and Miami Dolphins of the AFC. The Skins were led by a charismatic quarterback named Joe Theismann and a thirty-two-year-old fullback named John Riggins.

During the nine-game regular season that year, Riggins had gained 553 yards. But he wanted more work, and before the playoffs began, he approached Coach Joe Gibbs and brashly announced, "Give me the ball 20 to 25 times a game and we'll win it."

The coach took the fullback at his word, and in the three playoff games preceding the Super Bowl, Riggins got the football 98 times. And all he did was gain 444 yards, an average of 148 yards and nearly 33 carries a game, as the Skins whipped Detroit, Minnesota, and Dallas. He was especially effective late in the game, running the ball through the heart of the enemy defenses. Would he have enough left to do it again against the Dolphins?

Miami struck first, however, on a 76-yard TD play from quarterback David Woodley to receiver Jimmy Cefalo. The kick made it 7–0 and it stayed that way

Veteran fullback John Riggins of the Redskins runs right at the Miami Dolphins during his record-setting performance in Super Bowl XVII. The 32-year-old Riggins gained 166 yards for a new Super Bowl rushing record.

right through the first period. But the Skins were sticking to their game plan. Riggins carried the ball ten times in the opening session alone.

An exchange of field goals marked the opening minutes of the second period. Then the Redskins tied it when Theismann hit Alvin Garrett from four yards out and Mark Moseley kicked the extra point. But on the ensuing kickoff, the Dolphins' Fulton Walker rambled 98 yards for an electrifying touchdown. The kick made it 17–10 Miami, and that's how the half ended.

John Riggins had carried another seven times in period number two, and he continued to get the ball in the third session. It was getting to be his time, impact time. A Moseley field goal narrowed the lead to 17–13, and when the fourth quarter started, Riggins was ready to go.

Minutes into the final session, the Skins had the ball at their own 48. Riggins was called on twice and produced eight yards. Then Clarence Harmon ran for one more, giving the Skins a fourth-and-one on the Miami 43. They decided to go for the first down, and everyone knew John Riggins would get the ball once more.

However, he didn't do the expected. Instead of plunging straight ahead for the first down, he ran to his left behind a Joe Jacoby block. Then he suddenly cut outside with the move of a halfback, brushed past the cornerback, and was in the clear. Despite his 32 years and 230 pounds, the big guy could still turn on the speed. He outraced everyone some 43 yards to the end zone. Moseley's kick gave the Skins their first lead at 20–17.

After that, it was the John Riggins Show. The big guy kept getting the ball and taking it right at the Dolphins. Time and again he ran it up the gut and gained yards, as well as ate up the clock. He spearheaded a final touchdown drive that ended with a Theismann to Charley Brown pass. The Skins won the game, 27–17, and John Riggins had become a record breaker.

He carried the ball an amazing 38 times and gained a Super Bowl record of 166 yards. And he did it at an age when most running backs are either retired or seeing limited duty. Riggins, however, was still a heavy duty back. He was the MVP, of course, and he summed up his greatest day when he received a congratulatory phone call from President Reagan. After hanging up, a smiling Riggins turned and said, "Ronald Reagan may be President, but today I'm king."

Super Bowl record setters are often like kings. But, somehow, it seems the records don't last long. Seeing John Riggins gain 166 yards, many thought that mark would last for years. But you can drop the "s." It lasted only one year. That's when Marcus Allen and the Los Angeles Raiders came into Tampa Stadium in Tampa, Florida, to meet John Riggins and the Redskins in Super Bowl XVIII.

Yes, Riggins was back, and there was again a big focus on him. Could he produce another game like he had the year before? The Raiders' top back was Allen,

In the open field, Marcus Allen of the L.A. Raiders is as dangerous as any back in the game. He proved it in Super Bowl XVIII by gaining a record 191 yards on 20 carries. His 74-yard run in the third quarter was yet another Super Bowl mark, and one of the most exciting of his career.

who had just completed his second year in the NFL. But he had impressive credentials of his own.

In his senior year at the University of Southern California, Allen had set all kinds of records by rushing for 2,342 yards on 403 carries. He had a record eight 200-yard games and averaged 5.8 yards a carry and nearly 213 yards a game. He was the Heisman Trophy winner hands down that year.

With the Raiders, Allen had been outstanding, but only in spurts, since the Raider system didn't put him on center stage all the time, and he didn't get the heavy workload he had in college. But he was a fine all-around back, a six-foot-two-inch 205-pounder who could catch the football as well as run with it. And it was expected he'd play a big role in Super Bowl XVIII.

The Raiders struck first when they blocked a punt and recovered it in the end zone for a score. The point made it 7–0, and that's how it stood after one period. In the second period, Raider quarterback Jim Plunkett hit Cliff Branch for a long, 50-yard gain. Several plays later, he found Branch again from 12 yards out for another score. It was 14–0 when Washington scored on a field goal, but an interception and short return gave the Raiders still another score and a big 21–3 halftime lead.

In the third period, the Raiders continued to pour it on. Allen was having a good game, though he wasn't getting a large number of carries. Once they had the lead the Raiders began staying more on the ground. And Allen started to respond. Midway through the period, the Raiders finished a 70-yard drive as Allen scored from five yards out. That made it 28–9, as the Skins had scored earlier.

Toward the end of the period, the Raiders had the ball again, this time at the 26. Plunkett gave the ball to Allen who started running left. Suddenly, he was facing a group of Redskin tacklers. He stopped and reversed his field, running toward the right sideline. Then a hole appeared and Allen was ready. He darted through and was in the clear, outracing the Redskin defenders for a 74-yard TD run, the longest in Super Bowl history. He also put the game out of reach at 35–9.

Allen continued to pile up the yards. Late in the game, he scampered for 39 more to set up a final Raider field goal. When it was over, the Raiders had won it, 38–9.

And there was also a new Super Bowl rushing champion. Marcus Allen had carried the ball 20 times and gained 191 yards, averaging almost 10 yards a pop. He was the MVP for his outstanding performance. Later, Allen talked about his big run.

"I started by messing up the play," he said. "Then my first thought was not to get caught, and then I hoped there was no penalty. It was the best run I've had in the NFL. To tell the truth, I didn't think of what I was going to do. I just let instinct take over."

Instinct, determination, drive, and ability. These are the qualities that all the great ones have. This is what makes them record breakers. Marcus Allen has moved the Super Bowl rushing record close to 200 yards. So the next man who breaks it may just go over that magic barrier. But that's what records are for—to be broken. And a record-breaking performance is always a thrill to see.

# *About the Author*

**Bill Gutman** has been an avid sports fan ever since he can remember. A freelance writer for fourteen years, he has done profiles and bios of many of today's sports heroes. Although Mr. Gutman likes all sports, he has written mostly about baseball and football. Currently, he lives in Poughquag, New York, with his wife, two step-children, seven dogs and five birds.